"I nev— ...exually uptig—

The wo— ...provocative. Jake fought the impulse to kiss Michelle, even though she had just insulted him. "I'm not uptight," he said roughly.

Michelle arched an eyebrow. "So what are you doing on that bed when you're welcome in this one?" she asked, patting the sheet beside her.

Jake felt himself on the losing end of this battle. His pulse rate sped up. His throat tightened. And he wanted nothing more than to take her up on her invitation, consequences be damned.

Still, he had to try to gain control over the situation. "Respect. A gentleman never takes advantage. He…" Jake couldn't think when he looked at her seductive pose, so he shifted his gaze to her hands. "He gets to know her first— her likes, her dislikes, her favorite color… He gets to know her on an emotional level before moving on to the physical."

Michelle's generous smile caught him off guard. "I guess I haven't encountered many gentlemen." She went over and took his hands. "But Jake, why would you give a woman more than she's asking for?" Pulling him close, she whispered, "Don't you know that all I want is you…?"

Dear Reader,

Ah, those Magnificent McCoy Men! In the first
two books of the miniseries, *License to Thrill* and
The P.I. Who Loved Her, you met Marc and Mitch.
After these sexy-as-sin brothers, we thought we
couldn't possibly come up with another hero capable
of eclipsing their considerable shadow. Then out
stepped brother Jake...

In *For Her Eyes Only*, seriously single Immigration and
Naturalization Agent Jake McCoy bumps into fascinating
French national Michelle Lambert, and is thrown for
the loop of his life. Where he's conventional and rule-
abiding, Michelle's provocatively uninhibited and
willing to do anything it takes to get what she wants...
and near the top of her list is sizzling sex with Jake.
Will Jake obey the rules and keep her at arm's length?
Or is he man enough to see that some rules were
meant to be broken?

We hope you enjoy reading about Jake's seduction—
both in and out of the bedroom! And we'd love to hear
what you think. Write to us at P.O. Box 12271, Toledo,
OH 43612, or visit us at the Web site we share with
other Temptation authors at www.Temptationauthors.com.
Be sure to keep your eyes peeled for the next book in
the series, featuring delicious David McCoy, coming
your way soon!

Here's wishing you love, romance and many
happy endings,

Lori & Tony Karayianni
aka Tori Carrington

FOR HER EYES ONLY
Tori Carrington

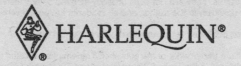

TORONTO • NEW YORK • LONDON
AMSTERDAM • PARIS • SYDNEY • HAMBURG
STOCKHOLM • ATHENS • TOKYO • MILAN • MADRID
PRAGUE • WARSAW • BUDAPEST • AUCKLAND

So many people, so little space! We wholeheartedly dedicate this book to everyone at Harlequin Books in Toronto for...well, for everything. But mostly for making it possible to do what we love doing most. Especially Birgit Davis-Todd, Randall Toye, Brian Hickey, Stuart Campbell, Katherine Orr, Stacy Widdrington, Maureen Stead, Carolyn Flear, Helen Higginson, Jennifer Tam, Meghan Dillon, Krystyna de Duleba, Amy Chen and—last but certainly not least, Brenda Chin without whom none of this would be possible. Thanks to all, named and unnamed! Without you, we'd still be writing stories that would make it no farther than our closet floor.

ISBN 0-373-25889-5

FOR HER EYES ONLY

Visit us at www.eHarlequin.com

Printed in U.S.A.

1

"JAKE, DO I EVER HAVE THE WOMAN FOR YOU...."

Jake McCoy tucked his chin toward his chest and squinted against the September morning sunlight. If any words could put the fear of God into him, those were it. Melanie, his younger brother Marc's new wife, had said them at the McCoy place last night—right after his other brother Mitch's new wife, Liz, took a perfectly good chicken and mutilated it beyond recognition for Sunday dinner.

His measured footsteps echoed off the asphalt of the parking lot across the street from the Immigration and Naturalization Service field office building in Arlington, Virginia. He hadn't responded to Mel's frightening proposition. Marc had answered for him, reminding his pregnant wife that Jake wasn't interested in a woman. That none of the McCoy men were. They had to be bitten in the ass before any of them would even consider the idea of marriage.

Jake had been embarrassed by the resulting laughter.

Then again, how was Marc to know how very close he'd come to getting married? Long before his younger, brash brother had even had his first sexual experience.

He tightened his grip on the files he held in his left hand, then absently moved his other hand to pat the breast of his jacket. Perhaps *close* wasn't exactly the word for his only brush with the M word. *He'd* been close. The woman he'd been dating, Janice Tollerby, was shocked when he'd pulled out the simple gold ring and proposed on their fourth date.

He still couldn't figure that one out. He'd known on their first date that he and conservative Janice could form a workable union. It was unimportant that he was new to the dating scene and that they hadn't known each other long.

For the first time he'd cut loose, taken a chance. And for the second time, he'd lost an important woman in his life.

He'd never taken a risk like that again.

He was a simple man, with simple tastes. He respected and appreciated routine, stability, discipline. He got up every morning at five-thirty, no matter what time he made it to bed. His need for simplicity was what led him to work for the INS. Those who didn't belong within the country's borders, or were no longer welcome, he sent home. Couldn't get neater than that. In fact, if not for his brothers, he'd probably never use any of his vacation time. It was difficult for him to justify leaving important cases in limbo even for a day. In an unpredictable world, he liked predictability. It comforted him to find the same selections in his refrigerator. When he replaced his furniture, he bought like pieces. And he had six identical dark brown suits in his closet. One for each workday, and an extra just in case.

His older brother Connor especially took great joy in teasing him about what he referred to as his anal tendencies. It didn't bother him. Well, most of the time, anyway.

It was a mystery still how David had managed to talk him into five days of hiking—hiking, for cripe's sake—through the Blue Ridge Mountains. With everything they needed strapped to their backs. Jake grimaced.

He patted the left breast of his suit jacket again. The familiar billfold holding his INS agent ID wasn't there. It hadn't been lying on his bedroom bureau that morning when he got up. And a thorough search of his apartment and car hadn't turned it up, either. He supposed it was possible he'd left it at the McCoy place last night, though not probable. There was no reason for him to have taken his ID out of the back pocket of his Dockers.

Then again, he wouldn't put it past one of his brothers to lift the sucker so he'd have to take his vacation, which officially started today.

Vacation. What David had planned sounded more like hell on earth.

He crossed the street, then looked at where his identification usually filled out the front of his jacket—and rushed headfirst into someone barreling in the other direction.

Jake didn't know how he'd overlooked the female who was pushing away from him. She had curly black hair and round brown eyes. Perhaps it was her height, which couldn't be more than five foot four to his six two. Or maybe it was her build, which was somewhere between skinny and petite.

"Excuse me," he said, running his fingers down the length of his tie.

She looked a million miles away even as she stared at him. In the bright sunlight her skin was a shade lighter than freshly milled paper, her lips colored a rich burgundy. She wasn't the type of woman he'd normally find attractive. Aside from the obvious contrasts in their sizes, she was too...tousled, as if she did little more than finger comb her dark curls. Curls that a light breeze tousled even further. And her mouth... His gaze fastened on it. Her mouth was too...distracting. Provocative.

Her gaze finally seemed to focus on him. She murmured something under her breath, then brushed past him in the direction of the parking lot.

Jake stood stock-still. He felt as if he'd just been sucker punched in a way he'd never experienced, and Lord knew he'd weathered his share of punches. He couldn't seem to draw air into his lungs; his knees felt ready to give out.

Slowly, he continued toward the building, wishing the

sensations away. He'd have to make a point to watch where he was going from here on out. He held open the door for a small group exiting the building. First item on his agenda: unload the documentation he promised to bring over from the investigations unit. Second: locate his identification.

Keys jangled. He glanced over his shoulder. In the lot across the street, the woman was unlocking the driver's side door of a battered old Ford. A once-over told him the tires were bald and he suspected she hadn't had the oil changed in the past ten thousand miles. His inspection also told him that she had incredibly shapely calves. And that she was probably much shorter than five foot four when she took off the impractical, thick platform heels she had on.

He caught a glimpse of a man walking in her general direction at a brisk pace, likely on his way to his own car.

Jake turned toward the door he held. No one else was exiting. A statute ought to be enacted disallowing women to have legs that looked as good as hers did. He caught the ridiculous thought. Well, at least they shouldn't be able to wear skirts that complemented those legs as nicely as hers did. It was downright distracting.

He absently patted his empty jacket pocket again, then slid another gaze at the woman's legs.

The man moving in her direction quickened his pace. Jake dragged his attention away from her long enough to figure out that the guy wasn't hurrying to get to his car, but was rushing for her.

He let go of the door, watching as the man knocked her over and grabbed her purse. Jake broke into a run, too far away to stop it from happening but close enough to catch up to the figure. The guy slowed to pull something out of the handbag, then dropped it. Jake swept up the purse, then lunged for the envelope the guy had taken, snatching it away. Their gazes locked. Just as Jake reached to grab him, the guy turned tail and ran. He disappeared into the depths of the city, the clap of his shoes quickly blending into the sound of car engines, blowing horns and a nearby siren.

MERDE.

The concrete pavement was cold and hard under Michelle Lambert's behind. She stared at a scratch on the driver's door of her car, her legs spread-eagle in front of her, her hair hanging in her face. After everything she'd gone through today, there didn't seem to be much point in moving lest she stumble into yet another nightmare. Yes. Better she should sit there. Breathe. Pretend what was happening wasn't. Wait until someone woke her from what had to be some sort of twisted sequence of events from an artsy, senseless independent film, the type that won awards in Cannes, not far from the town she'd grown up in in France.

Someone had snatched away everything that verified her existence: her passport, her plane ticket home, her money.

She forced herself to blink. Was it really just that morning that she'd discovered the manager of the crummy motel she was staying at had forgotten to give her her phone messages? By the time she'd called that swindling private detective she'd hired, he was gone for the day. His gum-smacking secretary had told her he'd need at least five hundred more American dollars to continue on the case. Dollars she hadn't had before her purse was stolen by some greedy, bloodsucking American.

She clamped her eyes shut. But the simple move wouldn't let her escape. She groaned, remembering her appointment with the INS mere minutes ago. The immigration officer's voice had been so clear, she could practically still hear it. *"Sorry, Miss Lambert, but we can't honor your request for an extension on your B2 tourist visa. You'll have to go back home to France tomorrow."*

Home.

France.

Without Lili.

She'd jump out of the plane window before she let that happen.

She opened her eyes, a foolish, tiny thread of hope winding through her. If she didn't have her passport, they'd have to let her stay, wouldn't they? At least until she could get replacement papers—

"Ma'am?"

Her gaze snagged on a shiny pair of men's shoes, then slowly drifted upward to a man's chest—a tantalizingly wide chest belonging to someone who towered over her like some sort of silent, handsome sentinel.

She looked into his face. "It's you." It was the man she'd bumped into earlier. The man who had large, slender hands and even larger calm gray eyes.

He held out her purse.

Michelle nearly burst into tears on the spot. "*Merci.*" She choked the word out in French, forgetting for a moment to speak in English. She rifled through the contents of her bag. Her passport. Her return plane ticket. Her compact, hairbrush, a snapshot of Lili she lingered over for a moment, multicolored receipts she'd accumulated over the past six weeks. Where was her money?

Her movements growing jerky and quick, she started looking through the contents again.

"Here." The man held her slender bill holder toward her. She noticed the way his gaze slid over her compromised position, his pupils huge, his throat working around a swallow. A bolt of unexpected awareness spiked through her as she accepted the money from him.

"That's all he tried to take," he said. His voice seemed to

come from somewhere very deep within him and vibrated right through her. "Are you...okay?"

Michelle pushed her hair from her face, looked where she clutched her purse in her lap, then stared at the run in her nylons. Her last pair of clean nylons. She felt like crying all over again. "No. I think you should just take me out back and shoot me."

His quiet chuckle drew her attention from herself and zoomed it in on him. He reached down. Michelle stared at his long, tapered fingers. Nice hands. Strong. Sexy. She placed her right hand in his, his strong grip lifting her to her feet.

"You hear about the crime, tell yourself you're being safe, you know, looking over your shoulder to make sure no one's following you. Checking the back seat of your car in case someone is hiding there. Double wrapping the strap of your purse to make it a difficult target. Then—bam! Some degenerate pig gets you anyway."

She sank her teeth into her lower lip. The more she babbled, the closer she moved to the tears she tried so hard to hold at bay. That's all she needed on top of everything else that had happened that day. To collapse into an unflattering pile of hysterical female in front of this very virile man.

She shivered at the undiluted heat that traveled from his hand to hers, only then realizing his fingers were still neatly wrapped around hers.

He cleared his throat, then withdrew his hand and patted the front of his jacket as if looking for something that wasn't there.

"You are an ex-smoker, yes?"

"Excuse me?"

She gestured toward where he patted his jacket. "I know many ex-smokers who keep the habit of reaching for a cigarette long after they've quit. My father is one." She slid the money envelope into her purse, then slung the strap over her shoulder.

"No...no, I don't smoke." He glanced away, as if caught looking at something he shouldn't be. Michelle glanced down. Aside from the run in her nylons and some dust on the back of her skirt, she supposed she looked all right. He cleared his throat again. "Shall I call the police? Or do you want to go to the hospital first?"

"Police?" Michelle's mind caught and held on the word. No, she definitely didn't want to waste any of the precious time she had talking to police. Every moment that ticked by was one more she wasn't using to find her daughter. "No, no." She lifted her purse for his inspection. "See, he didn't steal anything, yes?"

The corners of his sexy, generous mouth curved upward. "No."

"So no police."

"No police."

"Good." Michelle couldn't seem to tug her gaze away from his mouth. In every other way, this man appeared disciplined and ordered. But his mouth.... She ran her tongue along her teeth. His mouth looked downright delicious.

"Coffee then?"

"Coffee?" she repeated, blinking at him.

"Or tea." He seemed to grow inches taller as he straightened. "You, um, look like you could use a cup. You know, to settle down before you get back on the road again."

He nodded toward her hands. They shook slightly. No doubt the day's events were beginning to take their toll, but she didn't know how coffee or tea or anything with caffeine could remedy the situation.

He nodded to the right. "There's, um, a café a couple of blocks away."

His gaze was direct. His eyes clear. And just being near

him made her feel safe in a way she hadn't felt in a long time. In at least eight weeks. Before Lili was taken.

"Okay," she said quietly.

The man seemed surprised by her response, which didn't make much sense. Why should he invite her out if he expected to be turned down?

She followed him across the street where he picked up a manila file folder he must have dropped when he tore after the purse snatcher. He straightened the papers in it, looked at the INS building, then at her. "I guess I should introduce myself, shouldn't I? I'm Jake. Jake McCoy."

"Michelle Lambert." She thoroughly looked him over, thinking herself certifiable for agreeing to have coffee with this beautiful stranger, much less pondering all the other possibilities his nearness presented. But those same possibilities made her feel gloriously alive in a way she hadn't for a long, long time.

THREE QUESTIONS puzzled Jake. Who was this woman? What was he doing here with her? And why couldn't he shake images of her naked and moving restlessly beneath him from his head?

He sat across the bistro-style table from her, slightly turned to the side because he was too tall to sit as designed. Michelle Lambert took a generous pull from a latte, or at least that's what he thought she'd called it. She sat back with a satisfied sigh, licking the white foam from her upper lip in a provocative way that made him want to groan before he looked around to see who was watching. "It is not like mine, but it will do," she said.

Jake found himself running his tongue along his top lip, wondering not only how the foamy concoction would taste, but how it would taste on her.

He looked away. Everything about this woman seemed to

throw him for a loop. Her sweet, spicy scent was light, almost nonexistent, making him want to lean closer and breathe it in. Her accent, decidedly French, was heavy... sexy, which was a way he'd never viewed a foreign accent before.

He didn't know why he'd suggested coffee with her. He also didn't know why he was in the trendy coffee shop he must have passed a hundred times but had never entered. He glanced around the busy place. It seemed they served everything *but* coffee—at least as he knew it. He supposed part of the reason he'd extended the invitation was he couldn't see her getting into that car in the shape she was in. Besides, for a brief, telling moment, she had looked like she'd...needed someone. And he'd felt an inexplicable urge to respond to that need.

That he battled against a completely different need of his own was another matter entirely.

"Thank you," she said quietly, her small fingers curled around a cup that could have doubled as a soup bowl. "I...I really needed this. I haven't had a cup in six weeks."

He raised a brow. Six weeks? His mind clicked. He assumed that she hadn't had a cup of whatever it was she was drinking because she'd been in the country for that long. If that was the case, and if she was in the country on a B2 tourist visa, then it should be about to expire, if it hadn't already.

He didn't like his train of thought. Especially since it didn't seem to change his almost unbearable attraction to her one iota.

"My pleasure," he said in delayed response to her thank you.

She smiled. The action sent his stomach down somewhere in the vicinity of his knees. "You don't speak much, do you?"

"I've been told it's not one of my stronger suits."

"That's okay. I'm of the personal opinion that people, as a

rule, talk too much anyway. You know, when your friends tell you, 'I'd really like to go back to university,' or 'I keep meaning to lose that last five pounds,' my response is always that they shouldn't talk about it, they should just do it. Sometimes it seems the moment they say it, the importance attached to the statement loses all impact, you know what I mean? Anyway, how exactly do they expect you to respond? I think it's their way of asking you to share all those things you've been meaning to do but haven't, as a type of shared misery." She waved her hand. "I don't go in much for that."

He stared at her. He hadn't known a woman could say so much without taking a breath.

She smiled. "Then tell me what is."

"Excuse me?"

"You said talking isn't one of your stronger suits. What is?"

He noticed that her eyes were a light, light brown, matching the color of her designer coffee. He found himself returning her smile. "Well, I'd have to talk to tell you that, wouldn't I?" Her laugh was as smoky as he thought it would be. "Um, my job." Oh, but that was lame.

"Your job?"

"Yes." He didn't offer more. It was suddenly important to him that she not know he was with the INS. He was drawn to her openness. Her teasing smile. And he suspected that if she knew what he did for a living, she'd close all that off to him. He didn't want that to happen. Not yet, anyway.

He was relieved when she turned her attention toward the sugar decanter. She straightened it, then the napkin holder behind it, her gaze scanning the café's interior. "I once wanted to open a café."

His brow rose again, but for a completely different reason.

"Oh, not here. In Paris. Until Papa pointed out that the last thing Paris needed was another coffee shop." That smile again. She tucked her mass of unruly hair behind her right ear. Jake was inordinately fascinated with the move and found himself wondering if her hair was as soft as it looked. And pondered how it would feel trailing a path across the sensitive skin of his abdomen. "So I switched my plans to a restaurant."

Her laugh caught him unaware. What was funny about that?

"You know. If Paris doesn't needed another café, it needs another restaurant even less?"

"Oh." He cleared his throat again, then blurted, "You seemed distracted."

She squinted at him slightly, as if not understanding.

"When we bumped into each other earlier."

The light in her eyes diminished. "Yes. I was distracted."

She took another pull from her cup, and he looked at his own. He wasn't sure what it held. Was afraid to find out. "Any particular reason?"

He noticed then that she bit her nails. They were too short, barely crescents on her fingers. Unpainted. "Yes. There is a reason. Tomorrow, I'm told, I must leave your country full of swindling private detectives and bloodsucking purse snatchers. Go back home."

He held his gaze steady on her. Just as he suspected.

She gestured with her hands. "They, those people don't care that I need to stay here. That I need to find my daughter. They tell me they can't help me. They can't grant me an..."

"Extension." He finished her sentence.

She squinted at him again, making him wonder if she normally wore glasses. He scanned her features, imagining her with all that unruly hair pulled into a smooth twist—

"Yes, an extension."

"So you can find your daughter."

Her hands stilled on her cup. "Yes. Her father, or the man who calls himself her father when he didn't want any in-volvement in her life before now, came to Paris two months ago and…took her. Brought her here."

"Your husband?"

She shook her head. "No. He and I, we had a brief—how do you say it?—relationship. No, no, an affair. You use the same word, yes? Five years ago. He was an American living in Paris. I was a waitress. Lili was the result."

Jake stared at her. Not so much shocked by what she'd said, but shocked that she was saying what she was as easily as she was. And that he found it impossible to tug his gaze away from her animated face. She was a single mother who'd had her child out of wedlock. And she was *foreign*. Not that he had anything against foreigners. At one time or another, all Anglo-Americans had been *foreigners* to this land. But in his job as agent for the Immigration and Naturalization Service, the word foreigner took on a whole new meaning.

Not knowing what to say in the situation, he asked, "So your daughter's four?"

She briefly closed her eyes, her long, dark lashes casting shadows against her pale skin. She murmured several sentences in French. The thick, nasal sound wound around him in a way he wasn't sure he liked. It made him feel…lustful. He found himself wishing he knew the language so he could understand what she'd said, though he was sure it had nothing to do with his increasingly uncomfortable state. "Yes. She will be four this Saturday…five days from today." She stared at the tabletop, but he doubted she saw it. "I should have never given Gerald a copy of her birth certificate when she was born. I'd wanted to include him, yes? Instead, he used it to get her an American passport and take her away from me."

She looked so helpless at that moment. Much as she had in the parking lot when he'd returned her purse. He was filled with an inexplicable, urgent need to pull her into his arms. To smooth her curly hair. Tell her everything would be all right.

On the heels of that sensation followed a physical pull that left him feeling as if he'd downed a pitcher of beer in a single sitting.

The reaction was so completely alien to him, he wasn't sure how to respond. No one had ever stirred such a complete physical response in him. He had stopped paying attention to the countless hard-luck stories he heard on a daily basis about six years ago. Stopped counting the number of illegals he'd taken to the airport and put on the next plane out. Why Michelle Lambert's sketchy situation should affect him so baffled him.

"Have you visited the States before?" he asked quietly.

Normally he might not have noticed the slight coloring of her skin, but he'd been staring at her so much, any variation was noticeable. He wished he knew exactly what it meant. "Yes...I visited the west coast years ago. Vacation."

He grimaced. "So you're going home tomorrow?"

A waitress approached their table. "Can I get you two something else? A warm-up, maybe? The elephant ears are fresh."

Michelle waved her away. "No, thank you. I don't wish for anything more." She looked at him. "You've been far too generous already."

"Please," he said.

"No. No, thank you." She gathered her purse and got up. "I really must be going now."

Jake rose so quickly, he nearly knocked the table over. All he knew was a sudden, overwhelming urge to stop her from leaving. He curved his fingers around her arm. The heat that swept through him and pooled in his groin was instantaneous.

She gazed into his face, clearly puzzled. Then her expression changed. Her pupils widened, nearly taking over the tawny brown of her irises. The open sensuality he saw in the coloring of her cheeks, the softening of her mouth, made looking anywhere else impossible.

She slowly leaned forward, tilted her head and pressed her mouth firmly against his. Jake couldn't have acted more surprised had someone zapped him with a live wire, but he'd be damned if he could pull away. She tasted of chocolate and coffee. Smelled of fresh air and open interest. He wasn't sure, but he could have sworn he felt the quick flick of her tongue over his bottom lip before she pulled away.

He stood dumbfounded. Had that really happened? Had she just kissed him? His almost painful erection told him she had. And that he wanted her to do it again.

"Why...what did you do that for?" He barely recognized the low, gravelly voice as belonging to him.

She glanced quickly away, then gave a slight shrug. "Just curious."

"About what?"

Her gaze slid to his face, and she smiled. "Curious as to whether your lips felt as good as they looked."

She began to move away again, and he let her. Near the door, she turned toward him. "By the way, they do."

She stepped through the door.

Jake stood for a long moment watching her, an ache the size of Virginia in the pit of his stomach.

2

HE DECIDED to blame it on all the time he had on his hands. Jake stood waiting for the elevator to reach the second floor, only belatedly thinking he should have taken the stairs. And thinking of the prospect of having time on his hands. He'd passed his most pressing cases to fellow agent Edgar Mollens. His desk was clean even of dust. The only thing that stretched before him was five days trekking through the Blue Ridge Mountains with David.

He cringed. He'd be the first to admit that spending the night in a tent wasn't exactly his idea of a good time. In his mind, roughing it was being stuck in a hotel room without CNN. But even his reluctance to snap on his new backpack and tie his new boots wasn't to blame for his unusual interest in a certain provocative Michelle Lambert.

Then there was her kiss.

He forced the thought from his mind even though his body immediately responded.

At any rate, it was better that his chances of seeing her again were zip to nil. She'd never answered his question, but he was certain she'd be heading to France tomorrow. The elevator doors opened, and he stepped out. What he couldn't help wondering was when she was due to fly out.

Bypassing the administrative offices where he usually left any papers, he walked through the jam-packed waiting area in Room 200, vaguely aware of a number being called and an elderly woman likely of European descent using her cane to rise from her chair. He strode down the long hall leading to his office. His interest in Michelle should have been equivalent to his interest in the European woman. Less, even, because Michelle violated at least ten of his appearance rules.

Yet his mind kept venturing to her. The way she ran the small pad of her thumb across the rim of her cup while she spoke. Sat slightly leaning to the right, her legs crossed. Looked as if she could see inside him, appearing candidly interested in what was there.

Jake stopped outside an immigration information officer's cubicle and waited for the officer to finish with a young man presumably of South American descent. The kid finally left holding a sheaf of papers that likely reflected the details of his life thus far.

Pauline turned toward her computer, putting her back to him. "Good thing you're so tall, Jake, or else nobody would know you were there."

Jake entered the office. "What do you got on a Lambert, Michelle?"

Pauline entered the name in her computer. "French. Point of entry, Dulles. Extension denied." She swiveled slowly toward him. "Why?"

"Who handled the case?"

"Brad. You didn't answer my question."

"Thanks." Jake stepped out of the cubicle and headed to one down the hall.

"Jake McCoy, one of these days I'm going to cut off your special privileges. Then where will you be?" Pauline called after him.

He grinned.

Brad Worthy was between cases. Jake repeated his request for information on Michelle. Information that either hadn't yet been or wouldn't be entered into the computer.

Brad leaned back in his chair and tossed his pen to the desktop. "The Frenchwoman? Quite a looker, that one, eh?"

"I hadn't noticed."

"Yeah. You wouldn't." He shuffled through the files on his desk. "Extension denied."

"What else you got?"

Brad stared at him from under lowered brows. "What's the interest?"

Jake suddenly felt uneasy. He had a hard time explaining that one to himself. Maybe if he knew she was heading out, leaving for France, he'd be able to get her out of his head. "Indulge me."

"Okay." He opened the file and scanned the contents. "Lambert, Michelle. Twenty-eight years of age. Chef. Came in on a B2 tourist visa, though it's noted she tried to get a special travel visa. Claims her three-year-old daughter, Elizabeth aka Lili, was kidnapped by her biological father and brought to the States two months ago."

Jake digested the information. Chef. A transient profession. If she chose to violate the terms of her visa and stay in the country, she could find a way to stay indefinitely. "Why was her request for an extension denied?"

Brad sat back again. "She lied on her initial application about her criminal past. Information we didn't have when she came in but we since got."

Jake frowned as he recalled her vulnerability when her purse had been stolen. "Kid stuff?"

"Not this one." Brad shook his head. "Her visa's up at midnight tonight. But I can already tell you she's going to defy."

"How do you know that?"

Brad grinned. "Because she told me so. Let's see, how did she put it? That if I wouldn't give her the time she needed to find her daughter, she'd take it. Yeah, that's it. If she wasn't such a looker, I'd have had her detained on the spot." His grin widened. "Anyway, I'm planning to pass her file on to Edgar in the morning."

"Edgar?" Jake repeated. What could she have possibly done to warrant high-profile attention? He and Edgar Mollens took on the high-risk cases. Suspected terrorists. Drug runners. Russian Mafia. Sweatshop owners. What could Lambert, Michelle, possibly have done to earn the same regard?

And would her file have been passed to him if he wasn't officially on vacation?

He was about to ask for specifics on the conviction when Brad's phone rang. "Hang on a minute." He swiveled his chair away to speak to the caller. "Brad Worthy." Jake inconspicuously turned Michelle's file in his direction. The Four Pines Motel. He noted the address.

Jake's cell phone vibrated in his jacket pocket. He slipped it out and stepped closer to the door. "McCoy."

"How about that? There's a McCoy here, too."

Jake grimaced at the sound of his youngest brother's voice. "What is it?"

David chuckled. "You know, one of these days you're going to have to work on those phone manners, Jake. Then again, your entire demeanor could use a little work. Something I'm hoping to start on first thing in the morning."

"Are you at the house?"

"Yep. Thought I'd hang around until you got here."

"Listen, I can't find my INS ID. Have you seen it around there?"

"Can't say as I have. Boy, you must be feeling awfully naked. Anyway, I don't think you're going to need it where we're going, unless there are some illegal aliens hiding out in a cave or two."

"Right." Jake watched Worthy hang up the phone. "I'll call you back."

"Jake, don't you dare—"

Jake pressed the disconnect button and slid the phone into his pocket. Brad had closed Michelle's file and was motioning a new applicant to enter. That was it. Just like that, Brad had drawn their conversation to a halt. No more information. To press the matter would not only put him at a disadvantage, it would make his unusual interest in the sexy Frenchwoman even more obvious than it already was.

With a reluctant wave, Jake left.

"Hey, you're welcome, McCoy."

MICHELLE HAD NO IDEA why her extension request had been denied. If she had, maybe she could have done something to fight it. But the best she could come up with was that stupid situation she'd gotten herself into in San Francisco so long ago. Though why that brief period in her life meant anything to the American government, she couldn't begin to fathom.

She plucked her nylons and panties from the shower curtain rod, then stuffed them into her back pack on the double bed. She was blind to the crummy state of the room. The cigarette-burned carpet. The torn bedspread. The stained bathtub. Not because she'd been there long, but because in the course of the past six weeks she'd seen virtually identical rooms across the country. Truth be told, she'd lived in her share of such tacky places in Paris when she'd first struck out on her own. In Kansas, at least the rooms had smelled better, but North Carolina had to be the worst simply because of the bug population and the strong metallic smell of the well water.

The low-rent rooms were all she could fit into her budget. Actually, she'd have found they tested her budget if she'd sat down to think about it. The money she'd been saving to open her own place in Paris's Left Bank couldn't have run out faster had someone stuck a vacuum hose in her handbag and flipped the switch. And gone also was the additional money her father had wired to her two weeks ago. Of course, she hadn't expected her search to be so long, America so very large.

The mattress sagged pitifully as she sat on the side and tugged on her shoes. At least she'd finally gotten a decent latte, thanks to tasty Jake McCoy. In fact, she was thankful to him for much. If not for his quick reaction, she'd be sitting here with even less than she was now.

She absently rubbed her palm along her bare leg. And why had he reacted the way he had? In Paris, she'd had her purse snatched no less than two times, a third thwarted because she'd been determined, the thief careless. She'd been surrounded by people both times, but no one had lifted a finger to help. But Jake...

She sighed gustily, remembering her impulsive kiss and the masculine taste of him on her lips.

She wasn't certain which interested her more: the fact that she was thinking of someone other than Lili for the first time in so long, or that the someone on her mind was a man.

She pushed from the bed and smoothed the creases she'd made. Her mother had once told her, a year or so before she died, when Michelle was ten, that men were the one thing women could never live without. Michelle hadn't believed her. She'd forgotten the advice when she'd met Gerald Evans at the Jardin des Tuileries one rainy morning. He'd offered her his umbrella. She'd given him her heart, then, nine months later, a daughter.

She smiled wryly. Awfully high price to pay to keep a little rain off one's head. But she'd never looked back. Gerald had left Paris shortly after Lili was born. And Michelle and her daughter had forged a life of their own. A wildly variable life she loved. A laughter-filled life—shattered when Gerald had popped up two months ago.

She intended to get that life back.

A leisurely walk in the park with his daughter, he'd told Michelle. That's all he wanted. He was only in town overnight. Could she please allow him a brief time alone with Lili?

She had. And had regretted the decision ever since.

She rifled through her purse, extracting a sheet of paper. After leaving Jake McCoy at the café, she'd paid a visit to the private detective's office. Contrary to the information his secretary had given her that morning, John Bollatin had been in. And ten minutes later she'd left shaking with anger and clutching the address in her hand.

Canton, Ohio.

In a dusty corner of her mind, she remembered Gerald saying something about growing up in the Midwest. She had assumed it was Kansas. Going by the map, it should have been. And Bollatin had told her the same. But the address she held was in the northeastern corner of Ohio. An address for Gerald's parents.

She took out the billfold holding her money from her purse. She sighed at the pitiful amount, then slid it back in. She supposed she could call her father again, plead with him to send her more. But by now Jacqueline had learned about his sending her the other money and would have convinced him that sending more would be irresponsible. After all, they had three additional children to think about. It was an argument that had worked especially well on her father throughout Michelle's teenage years. And she had no doubt it was even more effective now, seeing as two of their children were still attending university.

No, she wouldn't put her father in that position. She was the only one who understood how devastated he'd been after her mother's death from breast cancer. It was as though a part, a very important part of him had died with her. Michelle took an odd sort of comfort in knowing that only she was aware of this. She didn't want to cause him any more pain.

Besides, living with Jacqueline and her three brats was enough for any man to have to bear.

No, she would have to find her way on her own.

And it was time she started. Now.

THE CAR'S TIRES spit up the spotty gravel as Jake pulled into the motel's parking lot. He put the gear in park, then shut off the engine. The sound of traffic zooming by on I-295 was deafening, making him wonder how anyone could sleep with all the racket. His apartment was located in Woodley Park, in the older section of D.C. Quiet, tree-lined. A bit of Norman Rockwell and old America in the middle of bustling downtown.

He stared at the closed door to Room Three. He couldn't begin to explain to anyone what he was doing there, much less come up with a rational explanation for himself. He'd tried already. It hadn't worked.

So what if Edgar was out of town until tomorrow, wrapping up a case in Georgia? Edgar was just as efficient as Jake was. And he had more years on the job. It didn't matter if he got the case today, tomorrow or the next day. Edgar would find Michelle quicker than she could blink those latte-colored eyes.

He shifted uneasily on the leather seat. The feeling was foreign to him. Very little made him uncomfortable. But not knowing what deeds lurked in the shadows of Michelle Lambert's past did.

At least that's what he told himself.

He shifted again, recognizing the statement for the lie it was.

He was drawn to this woman. It was as simple...as complicated as that. She ignited something within him impossible to ignore and equally foolish to pursue. But pursuing it he was.

He scrubbed his face with his hands. He realized part of the reason he was intrigued by her was that her reason for being in the country had nothing to do with finding a better job than she could back home. Or because she was in search of the American dream. She wasn't interested in any of that, as many foreign nationals were. She hadn't applied for a green card. She'd merely wanted an extension on her visa. So she could find her daughter.

There. There it was again. That bottomless feeling in the pit of his stomach.

And the image of Michelle sitting in a rocking chair with a dark-haired child in her arms. Her thickly lashed eyes sparkling with warmth. Smiling.

He left out of that thought the possibility that he wouldn't see her again. Despite that her beat-up Ford was parked a few yards away from him, she could have already skipped town. And knowing what she'd told Brad, he was convinced she would live up to her threat. There was a strength about her. A determination he couldn't help but be fascinated with.

His hand automatically patted his empty jacket pocket. He sighed, then slipped his cell phone out of his other pocket. Within moments, his father answered his call.

"Yeah, Pops, David around?"

There was the sound of clinking silverware. Jake envisioned the kitchen of the house he'd grown up in, finding some comfort in the familiar. Of course, so many things had changed since Mitch's wife, Liz, had moved in, but he chose to concentrate on those that had stayed the same.

"Hey, yourself, Jake," Sean said with that ever-present smile that had been in his voice lately. "He is. But are you sure you want to talk to him? He's mad as hell that you're not here yet. Not that I can blame him." There was a heartbeat of a pause, then his father's voice lowered. "It's not like you to be late for anything. Everything all right?"

"Just running a little behind." Jake grimaced. There were some drawbacks to having a family who knew him so well. He didn't doubt that if he were face-to-face with Sean, he wouldn't have gotten away with such a vague statement. "Any luck finding my identification?"

"Nope. Turned the place upside down earlier. Not even a fiber. Wait. Here comes David now."

Movement outside the car caught Jake's attention. Michelle was coming out of her room, a backpack slung over her shoulder.

"This better be good." David's voice filtered over the line.

Jake pressed the disconnect button then opened the car door.

MICHELLE SLUNG her pack onto the passenger's seat. This was it. All she had left was an address. Nothing more. And there were no guarantees that this address would be any better than the ones the detective had gotten before. She took one last look at the closed door to Room Three. But what choice did she have? She would not, could not go home without Lili.

"Going somewhere?"

Michelle turned at the sound of the familiar voice. Given how little he'd said to her earlier at the café, she didn't know why it should be familiar. It was more her body's reaction to the deep timbre than anything that told her Jake McCoy had followed her to her motel.

The funny thing was, she wasn't surprised by his appearance—maybe because she couldn't seem to get him out of her mind since bumping into him in the parking lot of the INS building.

She gripped the top of the door with her left hand. "Yes. I suppose I am."

He came to a stop before her. His back straight. His hair impeccably neat. His suit clean and pressed. She felt the sudden inexplicable desire to muss him all up.

"You wouldn't happen to be going to the airport now, would you?" he asked.

Her fingers tightened on the hard metal of the door. "Airport?"

"Yes. You know, for your flight home." He patted the breast of his jacket the same way he had at the café, then grimaced, as if not finding something that was usually there.

"No. No, I'm not going to the airport." She tucked her hair behind her ear. "What are you doing here?"

It occurred to her that he couldn't have followed her to the motel, because she hadn't gone directly there after they left the café. She'd stopped at the detective's office.

That meant he was either a stalker or else he'd known where to find her.

"Don't tell me. You work for the INS, don't you?"

He stood a little straighter, if that was at all possible, stretching that lean torso, drawing her gaze to his slim hips and legs that appeared muscular even through the light material of his slacks. "Yes, I do." He held out a business card. She took it, running her thumb over the raised lettering. Jake McCoy, Immigration Agent.

She closed her eyes and swore in French. "This day keeps getting better and better. Only I could meet a guy I'm attracted to for the first time in what seems like forever, kiss him, then find out his mission in life is to make mine miserable." She stared at him. "Does this mean *you're* taking me to the airport?"

He seemed to hesitate. "Do you want me to?"

She tucked the card into the waist of her skirt. "Do I have a choice?"

He glanced at a plain silver watch on his wrist. "Until midnight, you do."

She slid her hand from the door. "You have to be kidding." She regarded his clear, direct gaze and realized he wasn't.

"Have you eaten yet?" he asked.

"Eaten?"

"Yes. Supper."

She thought of the granola bar she had stashed in her backpack. With the meager amount of money she had left, she didn't have enough to splurge on little extras like food.

"Do you want to, you know, go catch a bite?"

"A bite?"

"Yes."

She crossed her arms under her breasts. On another woman, the move might have been provocative. Not with her. Like everything else about her, her breasts were small. Nonetheless, she watched his gaze skim the front of her shirt, the darkening of his eyes telling. Her nipples hardened beneath the thin, soft cotton, and a slow, arousing shiver tickled her spine. "Let me, um, get this straight. Isn't that how they say it? You're telling me you're with the INS. But you're not taking me to the airport. You can't. At least not until midnight. But you want to take me out to dinner. Is that right?"

He cleared his throat. "Yes."

She glanced at her digital watch. "It's only seven. Where were you planning on taking me?"

A glimpse of a grin played around his full lips. "I know this nice place that serves great French food."

She raised a brow.

"In Baltimore."

Her burst of laughter surprised even her.

There was no playing with this guy. He was as straight as they came. If she asked him how many times a week he took his suits to the cleaners, he'd probably not only answer her, but answer her accurately, down to the time of day he took them in.

She wondered if those same painstaking characteristics would make him thorough in his lovemaking, as well. He'd take his time. Explore every crevice and hollow. Make sure he was giving more pleasure than he was taking.

She caught her bottom lip between her teeth. "Sorry, but I've already eaten." She grasped the door again. "Thank you, though."

She climbed into the car, half expecting him to stop her. He didn't.

She rolled down the window.

He leaned over, his hands tucked into his pants pockets. "Mind if I ask where you're going?"

"No, I don't mind. But even you'd have to agree I'd be stupid to tell you."

He nodded. Her gaze was riveted on his mouth. While everything else about him bespoke discipline and order, his lips hinted at a passion she didn't think even he knew the depths of. She remembered the firm, silky feel of them against hers. His initial hesitation. Then his soft groan, and the confident pressure of his mouth as he returned her instinctual kiss. She could almost still taste him there, on her tongue.

She started the car's engine. "You're not going to follow me, are you?" The thought both excited and scared her, but not for the reasons she would have thought. While Jake Mc-Coy posed a threat to her freedom to find Lili, she got the distinct impression it was an altogether different autonomy he threatened.

Then again, one night with this man who looked at her in a mixture of wonder and desire might not be such a bad idea.

"Probably," he answered.

She settled on excited.

"Okay. Guess I'll be seeing you on the road, then."

"Yeah. On the road."

3

THE NERVE-GRATING CHIRP of the cell phone filled the otherwise quiet interior of the car. Jake fumbled in his jacket pocket then pulled it out. McCoy Place, the display read. He reached over and chucked the phone into his glove box. Until he saw what was going to happen over the next few hours, there was no point in talking to David. Michelle Lambert and her intentions took priority over a hiking trip. He glanced into the back seat, where all his new gear was tucked neatly into an oversize blue nylon backpack. The manager of the sports equipment store had told him everything he'd bought was top of the line. A sleeping bag no thicker than his linen bedsheets was guaranteed to keep him warm when the temperatures dipped below freezing, and dry when it rained for days on end. He leaned forward and stared at the sky. It definitely looked like rain.

He put both hands on the steering wheel and zoomed in again on the rusted Ford two car lengths ahead of him in the right lane. He was sure there was a law against the amount of exhaust the tailpipe was spewing out. And the wire holding her back bumper in place looked ready to snap. His gaze trailed to the open driver's window. Every now and again, tendrils of Michelle's curly hair trailed out and whipped in the wind. Like now. He watched her run her fingers through the unruly mass, casually gathering it on the other side of her head.

Jake adjusted the car's interior temperature. It was the first time he'd ever turned it past the sixty-seven-degree point. But that didn't bother him. What did was the irrepressible urge he had to turn the damn air conditioner off and roll his windows down. To feel the early evening air skim through his short-cropped hair like a woman's fingers.

He smoothed the front of his jacket and focused on the overhead sign coming up. Welcome To Pennsylvania. He'd driven this route before many times. Up through Maryland to Penn State, then either west to Pittsburgh or Cleveland or east to New York or Boston. When possible, he preferred driving to flying, and often times he got there faster on these shorter routes. They had yet to make a business-class airplane seat with enough leg room to keep him happy.

He relaxed a bit. The Pennsylvania turnpike was the only direct route through the mountainous state this far south. Not even he would attempt navigating off the four-lane thruway.

Off to the west, the sun was sinking toward the horizon, thin summer clouds throwing off shades of pink and purple. The vibrant colors made him think of the woman in the car ahead of him. Of her provocative nature. Of her small, round breasts. Her great legs. Her chattiness. His mind wandered, and he let it. As his doctor told him last week, there was no safer sex than mental sex. No one ever got pregnant or contracted an STD by indulging in fantasy. And sex with Michelle Lambert was—and would stay—nothing more than a harmless fantasy.

Images of rumpled bedsheets, an empty wine bottle and a Do Not Disturb sign on the door conjured a scene that made him squirm in his seat. She would be a talker in bed, that one. Pleading with him to touch her just so. Knowing instinctively just where to touch him. She would be insatiable....

Whoa.

Jake made a quick steering correction, then stared at his

lap. The last time he'd gotten a woody just *thinking* about a woman was when he was a teen. And he'd never indulged in fantasies about an overtly sexy, attainable female. While Farrah Fawcett had been his brother Marc's angel of choice, Kate Jackson always had been his favorite. Trim, neat, ordinary. Watching her in her high collars and conservative slacks had really flicked his switch.

Why, then, was he lusting after a woman who was a puzzling combination of Sophia Loren, Audrey Hepburn and va-va-voom Raquel Welch? One that went in for plunging necklines and short, short skirts? Didn't make any sense at all.

The wind caught Michelle's dark curls again, jerking Jake's mind to those bedsheets. They would be white and crisp, a contrast against all that inky black....

Tearing his gaze from the car in front of him, he pushed the button to turn off the air, then rolled the windows down.

JUST KNOWING Jake McCoy was behind her made Michelle feel erotically appealing. She'd never had a man literally pursue her before. Okay, his reasons weren't exactly what she'd like, but she'd bet his job wasn't the only thing on his mind.

She turned down the radio station cranking out rock and roll oldies, then gazed into her rearview mirror. She spotted Jake and his dark Caprice immediately. He never let more than two cars separate them and stayed for the most part in the left-hand lane, except to let others pass. How charitable of him. She caught herself smiling, then cleared her throat. She should be thinking of what lay ahead of her in Akron, Ohio, south of Cleveland. Instead she watched Jake. Noticing the way he held his hands on the steering wheel in the traditional three o'clock position. His correct, upright posture explained part of the reason his suit appeared barely wrinkled.

One hand on her own wheel, she reached down and plucked off her shoes, then slid them under her seat. Her speed let up a bit, and she instantly compensated. Jake did the same behind her.

The radio announcer told her it was eleven. Would Jake do as he'd said and take her into custody at midnight? He appeared to be a man of his word. Then again, if he'd thought her a real threat, he'd have stopped her from leaving D.C.

She focused more prudently on the road. It was completely dark. The only lights were her headbeams, which illuminated the monotonous, seemingly endless white lines that separated her lane from the next.

If Lili were with her right now, she'd be giddily trying to count those lines.

Michelle bit into the flesh of her bottom lip. It often seemed that everywhere she looked, everything she did, she imagined what her nearly four-year-old daughter would see or do in the same situation. Her absence was like a colossal hole, always present, forever threatening to swallow her up, bogging her down in the details.

What was Lili doing right now? Had she had her bath? Had she eaten? Did Gerald know that a certain name brand of baby care products irritated her sensitive skin? Or that he had to comb her hair just so to get out the tangles? Was she scared?

Michelle dragged in a deep breath. While she was fluent in English, Lili only knew a few basic words, and then only when used in conjunction with French. Would constantly being surrounded by the foreign tongue confuse her?

Oh, how she missed her daughter. Missed tasting her skin when she kissed her temple. Tickling her round, hard belly. Smiling at her rambunctious laugh. Missed playing hide-

and-seek with her and Julianne, her frazzled stuffed pet elephant and constant companion.

She reached out and took Julianne from her backpack, running her thumb along her nubbed belly, then lifting the toy to her nose. After nearly eight weeks of sleeping with the animal, it smelled more like her than Lili. But every now and again she swore she could make out her daughter's sweet, little-girl scent.

The sign ahead was blurry. She blinked, realizing that fog wasn't to blame for the haziness, but tears.

Stuffing Julianne in her temporary home, Michelle pressed her foot down on the pedal, watching as Jake dropped farther and farther back. Indulging in a bit of escapist flirtation was one thing. Allowing it to derail her plans was another entirely.

OKAY, SHE WAS finally making her move.

Jake flicked off the cruise control and eased his foot onto the gas pedal. He was mildly surprised she hadn't tried to shake him before. Then again, she might think being so far away from D.C. put them at the same disadvantage. Smart woman.

He easily caught up with her Ford, pulling parallel with her in the left lane. She flashed him a wide smile, making that peculiar weightless sensation more acute. He saluted her. But before he could put his hand back on the wheel, she slammed on the brakes then turned off the exit ramp to her right.

Letting rip a string of hardly used curses, Jake pulled to the shoulder of the road just on the other side of the on ramp, then flicked on his hazards. With his gaze glued to the rearview mirror, he slid the top button of his shirt open, leaving his tie to cover it.

Before Michelle had made her move, he'd kept a close eye

on the road signs. This particular exit had no rest facilities, and the next exit was twenty-two miles down the highway. Michelle would soon realize she had no choice but to get back onto the turnpike.

At least he hoped she'd realize that.

After five long minutes with no sign of the battered Ford, he jerked the car into reverse. Traffic was sparse, and he ignored the honking of horns from what little there was. He finally backed up far enough to exit, then raced toward the tollgate. The guard remembered Michelle—probably no other cars had exited since hers—and said he thought she'd gone east. Jake paid the toll then headed in that direction as well, scouring the dark farmland surrounding him. Nothing. No lights. Nobody driving. Nothing but a long, lonely stretch of two-lane road.

He drove for exactly three miles then stopped. He'd been had. It was as simple as that. He suspected that the instant she saw him turn off, she'd doubled back and was already well down the turnpike by now.

Then again, what she could be looking for could be here somewhere.

Trusting his first instinct, he turned around. He could only hope he was right.

On the turnpike fifteen minutes later, he saw that he was.

He pulled onto the shoulder then cruised to a stop behind Michelle's disabled Ford. The back left tire was flat. He climbed from the car and buttoned his jacket, careful of passing traffic as he made his way toward the driver's side.

No Michelle.

He leaned inside the open window. She'd left the keys inside. He used them to unlock the trunk. Why wasn't he surprised that there was no spare? A tractor and semitrailer roared on by, the resulting gust of air plastering his suit to his body. He stared down the road after the truck. Just then, it began to rain.

MICHELLE CLIMBED DOWN from the monster-size truck cab then slammed the door. There was a loud grinding of gears, then the trucker rolled slowly away from her, leaving her standing at the side of the road in the rain.

She shivered. It wasn't that she was unaccustomed to male attention. But the way the trucker had come on to her made her want to scratch something—that is, if she'd had any nails left with which to scratch. In France, men—no matter how old or attractive—at least hinted at the promise of or openly boasted of an ability to satisfy a woman. This guy had been moderately handsome, but he'd made it sound as if she'd owed him one. As though even if she wouldn't enjoy a sexual liaison with him, he didn't care one way or another, just so long as he could cop a feel.

Completely unlike Jake, who would probably never come on to a woman unless he were sure his attention was welcome.

She turned toward the lights on the other side of the tollbooth not too far away.

At least this exit included life of some sort. The one she'd pulled off in the hopes of losing Jake had been completely dead. She spared a glance behind her, half expecting to see the dark Caprice bearing down on her. Hiking her backpack a little higher on her shoulders, she headed in the direction of the tollbooth. She hoped they could direct her to a bus station or even a nearby train station, any place where she could curl up on a chair out of the elements, then continue on in her trip toward Ohio.

She hadn't counted on that flat tire. Then again, she hadn't counted on much of what had happened to her during her trip. She'd known when she'd bought the car that it didn't have a spare. It's how she'd gotten the dealer to go down thirty dollars on the price. She'd figured she'd gotten the better part of the deal, since the spare had been as bad as the rest of the tires. But even that would have been better than what she had now, which was nothing.

Headbeams illuminated her from behind. She stepped farther onto the shoulder as she walked. The way her luck was running, someone would hit her from behind, and she'd be stuck in an American hospital for the next month or so. Or, worse yet, in a cast up to her neck on the next plane to Paris.

She stepped up to the tollbooth. A woman in her forties eyed her critically. "Pedestrians aren't allowed on the turnpike."

"My car, it broke down—"

The attendant leaned forward and frowned. "I can't understand your accent, miss. Pass that by me again."

Michelle grimaced. "Is there a bus or a train station nearby?"

The woman apparently understood her. She leaned back and crossed her arms. "Nope. The nearest bus station is about twenty-two miles east, at the last exit."

Merde. She'd have to be careful, or the next thing she knew, she'd be arrested for loitering outside the tollbooth. "I don't suppose there's a cab service here?"

"Excuse me?"

Michelle shook her head. "Nothing. Thanks for your help."

JAKE FLASHED his high beams, then passed another eighteen-wheeler. He glanced at the truck cab. Michelle could have been in any one of the dozen or so such vehicles he'd seen in the past five minutes. Or in one of the cars, which easily doubled that number.

"What are you doing, McCoy?" he muttered to himself.

He gripped then released the steering wheel. His reasons for following her in the first place were shaky at best. And now that she had lost him...well, there was very little point in continuing without more information or an official reason for doing so. And since he had neither, he'd be better off turning tail and starting on the long road for home.

What had he been thinking? Or, more accurately, which body part had he let do the thinking for him? He grimaced. He'd never done anything so irresponsible in his life. When he was younger, he'd opted out of stealing candy bars from Obernauer's general store while Marc was busy stuffing his pockets full. Not because he was afraid he'd get caught, but because it was just plain wrong. Later, when Connor had surprised him with a stripper on his twentieth birthday, he'd handed her money rather than slip it in her G-string, and had kept his gaze carefully focused on a point just past her toned, undulating waist.

Why, of all times, he'd chosen now to let his hormones get the better of him, he didn't know. Especially since Michelle was nowhere near the type of woman he was usually interested in.

It stood to reason that that's exactly the reason he did find her so intriguing. But that didn't help him any now.

He slowed down to exit the turnpike so he could head in the other direction when the muffled chirping of his cell phone caught his attention. He reached over and fished it from a box of Kleenex in his glove compartment. He didn't recognize the number spotlighted in the display. Pulling onto the shoulder of the exit ramp, he clicked it on.

"Jake? It's Michelle."

He didn't need to be told that. Just her saying his name made his pants a little tighter. He closed his eyes and exhaled silently. It was weird, this physical reaction to her call. More acute than the first time he'd given his number out and the girl had called him.

Michelle told him where she was, then paused before saying, "Can you come get me?"

He knew how very much it must have taken her to call him. He also knew he shouldn't be feeling half the relief he was, either.

He glanced through the windshield at the tollbooth just ahead. He made out Michelle's silhouette instantly. She was leaning against the side of the booth, the toe of one platform shoe on top of the other as she plugged her opposite ear.

"I'll be right there," he said, then flicked off the phone.

Within moments, he was pushing open the passenger's door and paying the toll.

"That was quick," the guard said, openly interested.

He didn't answer her. He was more interested in Michelle as she climbed into the car and quietly closed the door. He pulled from the booth.

An air of defeat seemed to cling to her damp shoulders. Her sensual mouth was stoically unmoving, offering no babbling commentary on what the past half hour had held for her. She looked like a woman who had faced one too many disasters for one day and was ready to pack it in. He remembered who she was, who he was, and realized that the moment she'd called him, she'd done just that. She'd given in.

He fought a fierce urge to reach out and touch her. Pull her closer to his side.

"You about ready for that bite?" he asked instead.

She slowly turned to look at him. "Bite?" she repeated. "Oh, yes, food."

"I don't know about you, but I could eat a horse."

Michelle smiled. "Gerald used to say that all the time. Used to drive me nuts. Especially in the beginning, when I didn't know he didn't mean it literally. But why would anyone want to even joke about eating a horse? I mean, yes, I get the whole size thing...." She let the words drift off, her gaze traveling the length of him, then back again. The color in her cheeks made her eyes seem to sparkle.

He smiled at the reemergence of her chattiness, then wondered why the mention of size had caused her to look him over so thoroughly. "Gerald, your...ex-boyfriend?" He caught himself before he said ex-husband.

"Lover," she said, avoiding his gaze and crossing her arms. "And sorry, I don't frequent restaurants that serve equine animals."

"I'm afraid it's not an invitation."

Michelle closed her eyes, then looked at him. "Is it past midnight already?"

He nodded once.

"Then I'm suddenly very hungry. Ravenous, even. But I think I'll leave any horse they might be serving for you."

4

MICHELLE WELCOMED the vibrating hum of the hair dryer as she fluffed her freshly washed hair with her fingers. Her limbs felt rubbery. Her shoulders unbearably heavy. The long, hot shower had helped. So had dinner beforehand. At least what little she'd been able to make herself eat of the traditional American fare of meat loaf and mashed potatoes, the only selections available this late to her and Jake at the greasy spoon next to the motel. Even the tall, quiet INS agent who sat outside the bathroom door had appeared to lose his appetite as they sat across from each other. A pregnant silence had filled the air between them like so many unsaid, useless words. Unsaid and useless because Michelle knew that no matter what happened, Jake would be taking her to D.C. in the morning and putting her on the first flight to Paris.

She switched off the dryer and stared at the warm plastic in her hands. The steady drone of rain outside the slatted windows made it sound as though someone were taking a shower in the bathtub behind her.

She would be returning to France. Without Lili.

The thought that she might never see her daughter again caused a tightness in her chest that made it nearly impossible to breathe. What was she going to do without Lili crawling into her bed on rainy nights like this one, complaining about her inability to sleep, though she usually dropped right off once she'd curled her warm little body against Michelle's?

She supposed her life would come to resemble what the past eight weeks had held for her. Emptiness.

She caught a glimpse of her haunted eyes in the mirror, then reached out to wipe a small circle of steam from the surface.

A sound from the bedroom caught her attention. She realized Jake McCoy must have switched off the television. The tinny sound of voices was gone.

Jake McCoy.

Instantly, the tension in her chest unwound and snaked lower. She wasn't sure what it was about this man that affected her so. It could be his awkward way around her. His solicitous grin. The way he blushed—actually blushed!—when he found out they would have to share the one room left at the motel and when she caught him looking at her breasts. Or when she curiously eyed certain parts of him. Whatever it was, the attraction she felt for him was strong enough to, if not fill the hole left by Lili's absence, at least distract her from it a bit.

She cursed at herself in French. Six weeks in America and she was already beginning to overanalyze like an American. What was it with these people that made them question every feeling, every action, as if seeking a deeper meaning that wasn't there? She was used to going with her feelings. If it felt good, she did it. And the prospect of making love with Jake McCoy felt very good indeed. It held all the promise of complete and total escape, at least for a few brief, precious hours—enough to get her through the night and on into the morning, when her situation might not look so dim.

It would also satisfy the flash of desire she felt whenever he was near. Give her an outlet for the emotional turmoil dogging her. Allow her a physical release she'd forbidden herself for far too long.

She caught her tiny smile in the mirror, envisioning Jake's

reaction when she made her intentions known. Would he run for the door? Or would he surprise her with an equally interested response? Either way, she viewed it as a win-win situation.

She took body lotion from her handbag and began smoothing it over her skin. Her neck. Her breasts. The balls of her feet. No, she would not by any means be mistaken for a seductress. Her black camisole was pure cotton, and her panties were plain. But she didn't think even straight-shooting Jake McCoy could miss her message when she walked into the bedroom.

Fastening her attention on her hair, she smoothed it first this way, then that, frowning as strands sprang free like thick, unruly corkscrews. With the help of a little water and one of Lili's rubber bands she found in her purse, she managed to pull it back in what resembled a twist, every wild strand smoothed, tucked and pinned in place.

Her fingers encircled the doorknob and she hesitated— likely the first time she'd ever hesitated in her life. Why, she couldn't be sure. But in that one moment she knew a fear of rejection she was unfamiliar with.

Aside from their kiss at the D.C. café, there was no solid proof Jake was attracted to her. Yes, his gaze ignited the most delicious of desires within her. But her reaction could be based on nothing more than her need to escape the gravity of her situation.

She released a gusty sigh. There she went again. Analyzing everything too much.

She turned the knob then pulled the door open, standing in the passageway with only one thought in mind....

JAKE TURNED his cell phone over in his palm again and again. He really should call David, or someone at D.C. headquarters. But he couldn't seem to make himself do anything more

than listen to the sounds on the other side of the closed bathroom door.

He'd never been in such close quarters with a woman before. Well, yes, he'd been with a few women, and took some
amount of pride in the fact that they numbered more than
the fingers of one hand, but he'd never listened to one take a
shower before. The images that slipped through his mind
were just this side of pornographic and long past carnal. He
could practically see the warm water sluicing over Michelle's
compact little body. Dampening her hair. Rolling over those
soft, soft lips, tempting her tongue out to catch a drop or two.
Splashing over her pointed breasts, causing them to swell
and the tips to harden. He turned the phone over faster and
faster as he inserted an image of himself standing in that
shower with her. Bending down to claim her hot, wet
mouth—

The bathroom door opened. Jake lunged for his cell phone,
which had jumped from his hand.

Dear God, help me.

His gaze slid over her well-shaped frame. From the high-
cut panties that gave her legs the appearance of being ex-
tremely long. To the camisole that clung to her torso and her
breasts in a way his fingers itched to, to the way her hair was
slicked back from her face, emphasizing the width and depth
of her dark eyes, the fullness of her mouth, the long curve of
her neck.

She couldn't have provoked a more complete physical reaction from him had she walked out in nothing at all.

He forced himself to stare at the phone in his hands. "I put
your pie on the nightstand next to the bed," he forced himself to say.

She didn't move.

He didn't, either.

"Thank you."

He shrugged off her thanks and reached for the remote control. But the blasted thing refused to work. After a couple of moments spent futilely punching at the buttons, he tossed it onto the round, scarred table.

"I thought you could sleep in the bed closer to the bathroom," he said.

"So you could be closer to the door."

He looked up to catch her smile and felt the irresistible desire to smile back. "Yes."

She slowly crossed the room to the bed in question and began folding back the hideous bedspread. "I had another thought in mind."

Stick to her face, McCoy. Stick to her face.

She propped up the pillows on both sides of the bed. "I thought we might share one bed."

Jake nearly crushed his cell phone altogether.

She sat down and pulled her knees close to her chest. Far from the femme fatale her words implied, she acted as though she'd just suggested they engage in a long chat about the change in the weather. "Our being so...close would allow you to keep even a better eye on me."

Jake cleared his throat. "Um, yes, that it would."

"You object?"

He shook his head, then nodded. With a strangled sigh, he slipped his phone into his jacket pocket then pulled the jacket closed. "I find you very...attractive, Michelle. There's no denying that. But it would be..." *Unprofessional? Crazy? Decadent?* "It would be, um, imprudent for me to entertain ideas of you and I...well, making love."

He realized he hadn't even considered that this might be some sort of ploy on Michelle's behalf to gain her freedom. In his usually highly suspicious mind, he was notably unwary of her motives. Perhaps it was because of the way she looked at him, as though she was as interested in exploring the sparks that flew between them as he was. Or maybe it was the casual, unaffected way she invited him into bed with her. Either way, he knew, just knew on a deeper level he was hesitant to explore, that her desire to sleep with him was a result of just that—desire.

"Imprudent?" she questioned, the word rolling like melted sugar off her foreign tongue.

"Wrong," he said.

"Oh." She wriggled her toes until they were tucked under the white sheets. Her skin was as pale as the crisp linen, and appeared softer. "Because of your...job."

"Yes, of course, because of my job." Suddenly agitated, Jake stood. What he wouldn't give for a little of her chattiness right about now.

"I see."

"Good." He stepped to the curtains and pulled them back to stare outside. Rain came down in drenching sheets, making the night dark and intimate.

He watched her reflection in the glass as she got up and went into the bathroom again, then came out with her monster-size purse. Within moments, she was on the bed, propping something up on the nightstand next to the generous helping of cherry pie from the all-night diner next door. He slowly turned, finding her running a fingertip along the surface of a picture. Then she sat against the pillows and closed her eyes.

"Your daughter?"

She blinked and looked at him. "Yes."

He sat on the other bed and folded his hands tightly between his knees. The little girl looked nothing like he'd imagined she might. Rather than the dark hair and eyes he'd given her, she had straight blond hair that shone nearly white, and large green eyes.

Nearly four years old and she'd gone without seeing her

mother for eight weeks. Jake ran his hand over his face then rubbed the back of his neck. He'd been seven years old when his mother had died. And the days afterward, recovering from the shock, had seemed like months. Years.

Michelle propped her chin onto her bended knees and gazed at him. "Explain to me why your job makes it—what is the word that you used?"

"Imprudent."

She pressed her mouth against her skin. "Yes. Imprudent. Imprudent for us to have sex."

Jake shifted on the mattress, which reminded him that he was sitting on a bed. And that Michelle was sitting on another bed not a foot and a half away. He focused on his white-knuckled hands. "I could lose my job."

"If anyone found out."

"I'd know."

"Oh."

"Anyway, it's not in my, um, nature to sleep with someone I just met twelve hours ago."

"Eighteen."

"Huh?"

"We met eighteen hours ago. Remember? When we bumped into each other in the parking lot."

"Oh. Yeah. Eighteen hours ago, then."

She rubbed her cheek against her knee. "Why?"

He grimaced. "Why what?"

"Why is it not in your nature to have sex with someone you just met eighteen hours ago?"

He didn't miss her word usage. He'd described the possibility of their coming together as sleeping together. She'd called it having sex. He cleared his throat. And that's exactly what they would be doing, wasn't it? Having sex? They didn't know each other well enough for the word *love* to enter into the equation. He thought back, trying to remember if he'd ever done it. Had just plain sex. All six of the women he'd been with intimately had been longtime girlfriends, and he'd cared for them to varying degrees. But had he loved them? At the time, he supposed he had, which meant he'd made love to them, not had sex with them.

He gazed at Michelle. With all that wild hair pulled into that neat little twist, she looked different. More presentable. More like the type of woman he would be attracted to. Then why did he have the irrepressible urge to take it down? Watch it cascade down her back in silky, curly strands?

"Do you do that often?"

Her soft, feathery brows drew slightly together. "What? Have sex?"

He averted his gaze.

"Not nearly often enough."

He didn't respond. Couldn't respond.

"I haven't been with a man...well, since before Lili was born."

Over four years.

Jake didn't know why that should make him feel better. The woman had just suggested they climb between the sheets and have at it, and she didn't know him any better than the man in the moon. But he did feel better.

His want of her also shot up a hefty notch.

Michelle's lusty sigh pulled his gaze to her face as she leaned against the pillows and stretched her legs out in front of her. "I thought it couldn't be true. The rumor that Americans are sexually uptight. I guess it's the truth."

The word *sexually* came out sounding like a highly provocative suggestion. Jake fought the desire to stare at her mouth, though she had likely just insulted him. "I don't know that we're sexually uptight. We're just cautious, that's all. These are dangerous times we live in."

She shrugged, the movement making her small breasts jiggle under the cotton of her camisole. "That's what condoms are for."

"There's more than that to be cautious about."

"What? What is there that could possibly be important enough to keep a man and a woman apart when it's apparent they want each other?"

He was unable to tug his gaze away from her openly poignant one. She looked so unimaginably sexy, her eyes alight with fire, her mouth lushly challenging. "Fatal Attraction?"

Her burst of laughter was nearly his undoing. "You're talking about that movie, yes? The one where Michael Douglas's lady friend boiled his daughter's pet rabbit?"

He grinned. "Yes."

"Do you have a rabbit?"

"No."

"Then I can't very well boil it, now, can I?" She rubbed her toes against the arch of her other foot, her expression shifting. "Anyway, I'm returning to France tomorrow. There's no risk there, is there?"

He stared at his hands again. "I guess not."

"So what are you still doing on that bed when you're welcome in this one?"

Jake felt himself on the losing end of this battle. His pulse rate sped up. His throat tightened. And he wanted nothing more than to take her up on her invitation, consequences be damned.

"Respect," he said.

"Respect?"

"Yes. A gentleman never takes advantage of a woman. He..." He couldn't think when he looked at her, so he shifted his gaze to his fingers. "He, um, gets to know her first—her likes, her dislikes, her favorite color, things, um, like that. Gets to know her on an emotional level before moving on to the physical."

Her generous smile caught him off guard. "That's the most I've heard you say all at once. This subject must really bother you."

He shrugged his tense shoulders. "It's the way I was raised."

"But why give a woman what she isn't asking for?"

He didn't answer her. God, she was forthright, wasn't she?

Her head lolled on the pillow. A few strands of dark hair broke free and drifted to lay across her cheek. "Okay, then. Things I like. I like the feel of the sun on my face when it's just risen over the horizon. I like it when I'm in the kitchen cooking, experimenting with new flavors." Her voice dropped an octave. "I like holding my daughter after she's been outside, smelling the fresh air in her hair, on her skin."

Jake's gaze drifted to the picture on the nightstand.

"My dislikes. I don't like when the shower runs out of hot water when I still have shampoo in my hair. I don't like new shoes when they're too tight and need to be broken in." She bit briefly her bottom lip. "I don't like that I can't hear my daughter's deep breathing as she sleeps."

Silence settled over the shadowy room. He'd asked the questions. He didn't know why her answers should affect him so.

"My favorite color is purple."

He looked up to find her smiling. "Purple?"

She nodded. "Now you go."

Jake's stomach tightened. He'd said he wanted to know those things of the women he dated. He hadn't mentioned sharing those answers with them.

"You like...?" Michelle prompted.

"I like..." His words drifted off.

She waited, her head resting against the white pillowcase. "Why don't you start with your dislikes? It might be easier."

"Okay." He paused, thinking. "I dislike..." His mind

went completely, totally blank. This was a unique situation for him. Not his reluctance to speak—he'd always been conservative with words. But Michelle's interest in his thoughts threw him for a loop.

"You want me to try for you?"

He nodded slowly, relieved by the reprieve, curious as to what she'd say.

Michelle sat up cross-legged. Jake fought the desire to look at her lap, at the way her panties were likely stretched across her feminine parts. "Okay, Jake McCoy, this is how I see you."

He smiled, wondering just how much she thought she knew about him in such a short period of time, and what he'd say when she was wrong.

"You don't like to step outside your box."

"Box?"

"Yes...your comfort zone. You like things the way you like them, and you don't like change."

He stared at his hands.

"You obey a set of internal rules—"

"What do you know about rules?" he asked a little too abruptly, unaware he'd felt so vehemently about her apparent lack of them, and uncomfortable of her awareness of his truckload full.

She sat silently for a moment, gazing at him. "I know plenty about rules." She rubbed her palm against her leg absently. "It's rules that will cut short my search for my daughter. It's rules that have you on that bed, me on this one." She hopelessly tried to smooth stray tendrils of hair into the twist. "No one actually likes stepping outside their box, Jake."

"You seem to do it easily enough."

"Only because I have to."

He narrowed his eyes. "You have to sleep with me?"

He watched her slender neck contract as she swallowed. "I want to sleep with you."

"So what is it you *have* to do?" he asked.

Her voice was so low it was almost a whisper. "I have to find my daughter so I can go back to my life the way it was."

Jake paused. Interesting. He was just thinking his life had truly yet to begin.

She worried her bottom lip between her teeth, then sighed. "All right. Enough of your dislikes. You obviously dislike anyone guessing anything about you. Why don't we go back to your likes?"

"My likes?"

She nodded.

Well, he'd better get on with it, or she'd likely offer answers for him. And he didn't know if he could bear her guessing so accurately.

"I, um, I like the smell of hay when it's just been cut," he said haltingly.

Her brown eyes warmed. "Good. That's good. I like that, too. You must have been born in the country, like I was."

Too bad those countrysides were in different parts of the world, Jake thought. He caught the errant thought and went on. "I like the taste of roast beef straight from the oven. You know, when it melts on your tongue like gravy." He coughed. He'd be the first to admit, he never went beyond what was absolutely necessary to get his point across. So what was with that gravy bit?

He expected to see amusement in her eyes when he looked at her. Instead, he saw a simmering heat that caused a responding spark to ignite in his groin.

He didn't quite know what it was about this woman that made him feel different, made him want to act on impulses he might not even have noticed before. He traded the side of his bed for hers, and hesitantly cupped the side of her face.

She uncrossed her legs and leaned into his touch, her lashes fanning across her cheeks.

He eyed her mouth, torn between wanting to kiss her and needing to pull away. "I, um, like you."

Like wasn't even the word. He *burned* for her. If he couldn't take her right now, bury himself in her slick, hot flesh, he felt like he'd die. Right then and there. He couldn't remember a time he'd wanted a woman so passionately, so desperately. Above and beyond everything he knew was right and made sense. All he knew was an obsessive need to possess her.

He inexpertly pressed his lips against hers. Testing her. Testing himself. Then all thoughts of right or wrong, awkwardness or skill deserted him, and he branded that lush mouth of hers with a kiss so hot, even she widened her eyes briefly before curling into him, opening to him, moaning in obvious relief and desire.

Maybe she was right. Maybe there were times when just plain sex was called for.

He reached up and tried to take the band from her hair. She made a soft little sound, telling him he must have hurt her. He began to pull away.

"Sorry."

"No, no, it's okay."

Catching his hand, she freed her hair for him. He carefully shook the pins out with his fingers, reveling in the silken feel of her curls as they cascaded around his hands and wrists, teasing the skin there. He tangled his tongue with hers, unable to taste near enough, fast enough for his liking.

There was that word again. Like. He liked her responsiveness. He liked the way she arched against him, the pointed tips of her breasts pressing against his starched white shirt. He liked the sound of her soft moans, her shallow breathing as she pushed and pulled at his jacket, getting it halfway down his arms, essentially pinning him, before moving to the buttons of his shirt.

Oh, how he liked giving himself over to something greater than his internal code of conduct. It felt...indecent. Demanding. Liberating.

He clumsily shrugged the remainder of the way out of his jacket, then his open shirt and bunched-up T-shirt. Michelle immediately pressed her hot palms against his flat nipples, then followed with her tongue, nipping at his sensitive flesh with her teeth, then sucking him deep into her mouth.

Jake groaned, then grasped her upper arms, claiming her mouth once again as his. Delving his tongue deeply into the wet recesses, skimming the smooth enamel of her teeth, pulling her tongue into the depths of his.

She tasted of toothpaste and mouthwash, warm skin and soap. She tasted of things forbidden, things denied. She tasted of hungry female to his needy male.

He wasn't sure how it had happened—whether she had done it or he had done it, or if they had done it together—but he was suddenly undressed. His erection pulsed against the skin of his abdomen, ramrod straight and aching. And Michelle was straddling his lap, staring at him with such incredible longing in her eyes he was afraid it would end before it had even begun.

Hesitantly, Jake ran his hands up the velvety skin of her belly, inching her camisole up and then over her head. He caught his breath at the sight of her, then gently cupped her breasts in his palms. They were the perfect size for her height, with large, upward tilting nipples the color of warm honey. He ran the length of his tongue against one, watching as it tightened into a thick nub. He'd never been so turned on by the mere sight of a woman's breasts before. But Michelle's... They encompassed all that she was: small, saucy, provocative and so very, very sexy.

He thoroughly laved first one, then the other, his motions starting out slow, then growing quick, impatient, until he hungrily pulled at her stiff nipples, his hands restlessly traveling over her molten skin, then down to rest on her outer thighs.

Her voice, when she spoke, was soft and husky, "Yes... yes. Touch me...there."

He closed his eyes and muttered a curse against her temple, then drew back as he slid his fingers inward toward the swollen folds pressing against the soft cotton of her panties. Ever so gently, he skimmed his thumb in the shallow crevice, feeling the dampness of her need and her violent shudder. She tried to squeeze her legs together, but he held them open, then tugged the crotch of her underwear aside, baring her curls to his sight.

She whispered something in French. The sound of the thick, unintelligible words drove him mad with longing as he kissed her again and again. She ground her pelvis against his touch, seeking something he feared for a moment he couldn't give her. Then she reached for his erection, rolled on a condom he vaguely remembered taking out of his wallet, then eagerly guided the hooded tip to her slick opening.

Jake was helpless to do more than watch as she lifted herself up onto her knees, then slowly took him into her, inch by torturous inch.

"Oh, God." She was so exquisitely snug and wet, fitting over him like a too small glove. Sweet, agonizing pleasure broke over him, clenching his muscles, contracting his chest until he could do little more than let her take the lead.

And take the lead she did. Much to his surprise, she took every last millimeter into her compact little body and remained perfectly still, as if allowing her muscles time to adjust to the difference in their sizes. Then she rocked her hips forward.

Jake groaned and grasped her hips. If he...if they...if she continued, he'd be a goner in no time at all.

Michelle hungrily ran the tip of her tongue along the seam of his mouth then drew his lower lip into her mouth. "You, um, never told me what your favorite color is," she murmured, then moaned when he thrust upward into her sweet flesh.

What was she talking about? Oh, yes. His favorite color.

He plucked her from his lap and laid her across the sheets, then covered every inch of her skin with his before lifting her right knee and plunging deeply into her with one long, urgent thrust.

Gone were all the barriers that separated them. He was no longer an INS agent. She was no longer an illegal alien. He was no longer a man who had a difficult time identifying and expressing his emotions. She was no longer a woman with problems he couldn't hope to understand. They were simply a man and woman, giving themselves over to the most fundamental of human needs.

He absorbed her shudder and drank her cry into his mouth as he kissed her. He slowly withdrew, then thrust again...and again, until red colored the backs of his eyelids.

"Red," he said between clenched teeth, sliding his hands under her behind and tilting her hips upward. "My favorite color is red."

Then his world exploded into multifaceted spears of the brilliant, vibrant color.

5

SOMEHOW even the rain looked different. Fantastical.

Fantastical? Jake hated the rain.

But this morning all he could do was sit inside the car and stare out the windshield at it, wearing a silly grin.

Last night was...incredible. Hot. Just thinking about it gave him a hard-on. Maybe all this—his near obsessive attraction to Michelle, his preoccupation with her whereabouts, her tight little body—had been about his need to get laid, and laid properly. Giving in to Michelle's request for just plain sex, without commitment, had been one of the best things he'd ever done. He'd never felt so...free in his life. He wanted to get out of the car and stand in the rain, feel it roll down his face and into his mouth, drench his clothes. And usually, unless it had something to do with a shower, he hated getting wet.

Last night had nothing to do with giving. It had been all about take. He'd touched her breasts not to give her pleasure, but to see if they were as pliant as they looked. He'd plucked at her nipples, not to illicit her moan, but to test the erect peaks. He'd grasped her hips not to guide her, but to grind into her. He'd never done that with a woman before. He'd always been hesitant, more concerned with how the woman would like to be touched than how he would like to touch her.

And Michelle...

His erection grew. He groaned in a mixture of pleasure and pain.

Michelle had to be one of the most uninhibited women he'd ever known. She hadn't cared that the lights were on. Had no interest in pulling the blankets up to her chin to block her skin from view. She'd been gloriously proud in her desire. A powerful aphrodisiac, that, watching a woman throw her head back in abandon and stroke herself up and down on his manhood.

"Cripes."

Jake flicked the fan on high. If he didn't stop this, he'd march right into that motel room and take her all over again. And knowing she'd likely be as open to the proposition as he was made it that much more difficult not to.

He hadn't known what to expect when he woke up that morning. He'd stared at the water-stained ceiling, then nearly hit the ceiling when he realized where he was and what he had done. But then he'd turned his head and found Michelle snoring lightly, her bare behind pressed against his side. She hadn't been in the bathroom getting dressed, putting distance between them. No. And her demeanor had remained the same after she awakened. No morning regrets. No coy remarks or shy smiles. She'd yawned, thrown him a sexy, sleep-softened smile over her shoulder, then burrowed further against him.

Jake had been completely floored.

He hadn't known women like Michelle existed. Well, that wasn't entirely true. What he hadn't known was that everyday normal women like Michelle could be so...sexually generous.

That was normally a man's approach, wasn't it? Not that he had ever experienced casual sex before. Even his first time had been with a girl from town he'd known since kindergarten and had courted his entire life. Both he and Mary Beth had sat in the barn afterward wondering if that's all there was.

Oh, no, baby, that definitely wasn't all there was. There was...there was....

There was Michelle.

He watched the door to Room Twelve open, and his erection popped to life again. She'd changed into a pair of stretchy black slacks and a close-fitting white top. She gave the rain a noting glance, then stepped toward the car without rushing, without using her bag to shield her from the rain. When she climbed in, the scent of shampoo from her damp hair filled the interior. It was all Jake could do not to draw the smell in with a deep breath.

He backed out of the spot and headed for the turnpike.

"Michelle, I..."

She looked at him. "Yes?"

He shrugged, then flicked his gaze to the road. "I just felt...think I need, you know, to say something to you about last night...."

She scooted so that her left knee was curved on the seat and she was half facing him.

He couldn't help his grin. "It was...incredible."

Her husky laugh sent a burning sensation through his veins. "Yes, I'd say last night rates up there on the incredible level." She glanced away.

Jake gestured with his right hand. Catching himself, he snapped it onto the steering wheel. "I mean...what I'm trying to say is... Oh, hell, I don't know what I mean."

And he didn't. He'd just wanted to acknowledge what had passed between them. And her sexy little smile told him he'd not only accomplished that, but that she felt the same. "So you don't regret it?" she asked.

He stared at her wide-eyed. "Regret it? Hell, no, I don't regret it." He grimaced at the vehemence of his words. God, he must sound like a nineteen-year-old who'd just experienced his first blow job. "This morning, though, I thought for a minute that maybe you had. Regretted it, I mean."

She shook her head, her curls bouncing around her shoulders. "Not me."

"Good."

Her smile widened. "Great."

"Yeah, it was great, wasn't it?"

She laughed, and he realized he was pretty much repeating himself at this point. Was he really jabbering? Him? Big, silent Jake McCoy? He couldn't count the number of times his brothers had tried to force him to talk. Often when they were younger, Connor used to pin him down, trying to get him to spill something or other. But he never had. Now he was not only offering stuff up voluntarily, he was repeating himself. Go figure.

After a few moments of silence, Michelle looked at him again. But the serious expression on her face chased every single light, sexually charged thought from Jake's mind:

"Jake, I..."

For the first time, he noticed the slight smudges under her dark eyes. While a current of electricity still crackled between them, it was obvious her mind was on something else. More specifically, the fact that he would be sending her back to France.

Jake mentally ground out a curse. It wasn't that he'd forgotten about that small little detail. Oh, hell, who was he kidding? He had purposely shoved aside the fact that she was officially an illegal alien, and he was an INS agent. Another first for him in this recent slew of firsts. Now the weight of reality pressed in on him from all sides.

Michelle straightened her legs and stared out the passenger window.

"Were you going to say something?" he prompted.

She shook her head. "No...nothing."

He cleared his throat and turned his gaze toward the windshield. The emotional turnaround hit Jake like a two-by-four to the head. So occupied was he with the uniqueness of last night, of Michelle's generous nature, her innate sexuality, he'd completely lost sight of exactly where they were and why.

Not anymore.

He should have gotten out and stood in the rain. Maybe it would have woken him up long before now.

MICHELLE'S MUSCLES felt thoroughly worked out, stretched, pulled and sated. She stared out the window at the passing mountainside and absently touched her slightly swollen lips. She tried to keep reminding herself that this was a solemn occasion. She was being taken back to D.C., where she would be placed on a plane for France, her search for Lili abruptly cut off. But all she could do was think about how she had suggested casual sex with Jake the night before, and how there had been nothing casual about it.

She wasn't sure what it was about this man. He was tall, quiet, wholesome. And she'd loved messing him up. It wasn't so much him that concerned her, but her reaction to him.

She'd had attentive lovers before. Men who knew exactly how and where to touch her to bring her pleasure. Men with far more experience than Jake McCoy. But there had been something substantially different about the way he had responded to her. A hunger in him, a fascinating agility and a capacity for deep emotion that had rocked her down to her toes. When he'd cupped her breasts, she'd nearly climaxed right then and there. Not even when she was younger had she been so easily pleased. There was something about the look in his eyes, the heat of his fingers, the sound of his quiet groans, that had turned her inside out in a way she'd been completely unprepared for.

Never, never had anyone stirred her the way he had.

Michelle leaned her forehead against the steamed glass of the window and tightly closed her eyes. She'd once pondered the difference between sex and genuine lovemaking. But she'd stopped that long ago. She'd come to the conclusion that there was sex and great sex, and that great sex must have been what others called lovemaking.

No longer. As foolish as it was, she knew, deep in her bones, that what she and Jake had done last night was made love.

"Merde."

The sound of the windshield wipers reminded her where she was, as did Jake's question. "Pardon me?"

She turned toward the sound of his voice, goose bumps peppering her skin. "What?"

He lightly shrugged, a sexy grin tugging at the sides of his mouth. "I thought you said something."

"No. No. Nothing."

He fell silent again.

Michelle took the opportunity to study him. Really study him. Wasn't it odd that after knowing the man for only a day she should be so comfortable with him in silence? She was a born talker. At least that's what her father used to say when she would come home from school and tell him moment by moment exactly what had happened to her that day. Why then should she be perfectly content, invigorated even, sitting next to Jake McCoy and feeling no need to say anything?

Oh, God, she was in over her head here.

Which was ridiculous, because tomorrow at this time, she'd be in Paris, half a world away, and Jake and last night would seem even farther away.

And so would Lili.

Guilt, quick and consuming, enveloped her.

Jake made a quick swerve into the right lane, then to the off-ramp. Michelle had to grab the dashboard to stop herself from colliding with him.

"What is it? What's wrong?" she asked, staring at the approaching tollbooth.

"Change in plans, that's all," he said, looking as shocked as she felt. "We're going to take the scenic route back. Through Ohio."

Her heart skipped a beat. Had she heard him right? Had he just said they were going to Ohio? Ohio was where Lili was. And far from being on their way to D.C., it was completely out of the way.

She didn't dare speak for fear that his response would prove she was imagining things.

He glanced at her as he paid the toll, then headed over the bridge and onto the turnpike going west. "That's where you said Lili was, right?"

She nodded slowly, her entire body trembling.

He shrugged, though there was nothing nonchalant about the move. He appeared determined somehow. Serious.

"Jake, I..." she began again for the second time in as many minutes.

"What is it?"

She bit her bottom lip and sighed. "Look, I don't want you to think that you, you know, need to do this because of what happened last night."

He glanced between her and the road several times, then his eyes widened. He looked so endearingly shocked, she nearly laughed. "You mean like as some sort of...favor for a favor?"

She gestured with her hands, trying to pull the right words out. Instead, she settled for a simple yes.

"No," he said.

"Are you sure?"

"Of course I'm sure." She watched his hands tighten on the steering wheel. The same hands that had given her such pleasure only hours before. She shivered. "Look, Michelle, I don't know what you're used to, but this has nothing to do with...you know, our having had sex."

She couldn't help her smile. "Good."

"Great." He grimaced, then shrugged again. "I just, you know, thought that it wouldn't be that big of a deal to go to Ohio, see if this lead you have pans out, before heading back to D.C., you know?"

She really hated to argue with him. After all, he was doing exactly what she would have wished for, if she had dared to wish. "But won't you get in trouble?"

His grin nearly swallowed his handsome face. "Only if anyone finds out."

THREE HOURS LATER, they rolled over the Ohio line. Jake squeezed the steering wheel. He didn't know quite how to explain this. One minute he'd been driving Michelle to D.C. The next he'd been making a U-turn.

She hadn't had to say a word. Hadn't pleaded with him to give her a little while longer. Hadn't played on his conscience about how important a role a mother had in her young daughter's life. No. He'd been the one to silently say the words. Perhaps that's why he'd made the decision himself.

Or maybe it had more to do with the small, ragged elephant he'd found lying on the bed while Michelle showered that morning.

His knuckles whitened. Or perhaps he was way off with both explanations and he was just looking for an excuse to have her in his bed for another night.

"So many roads," Michelle murmured.

He glanced to find her bent over the map, the sunshine slanting through the window igniting the blue highlights in her curly black hair. Funny, but no sooner had he turned the car west, than the storm clouds had parted. It was difficult to tell it had rained at all.

Michelle crowded her fingers into all that hair and swept it to the other side of her head. She looked at him. "We want to take route—"

Her words abruptly broke off, and the shadow of a smile lifted her lips. "What?"

Jake realized he was staring, but was helpless to stop between glances at the road. "Your hair. I like it better down."

"Oh." He noted the slight coloring of her cheeks before she turned toward the map spread across her lap.

Had she just blushed? Jake concentrated his attention on the road. Twenty-four hours ago, he'd have sworn nothing was capable of making a ballsy woman like Michelle Lambert blush. Yet she just had. And he had been the cause of it, or at least his spontaneous compliment had. Out of the corner of his eye, he watched her settle her hair around her face.

"Route forty-three." The rustling of paper sounded as she repositioned the map and following a red line with her index finger. "It should be coming up in a few kilom—miles, I think."

"This PI you hired. How sure was he that Li—your daughter is here?"

Michelle slowly folded the map, the hope momentarily draining from her face. "I don't know. I thought he was sure when we went to Kansas last month, then to North Carolina last week." The map crinkled where she held it too tightly.

Jake was filled with the sudden urge to track down the slimy PI and have at him. Not to mention his desire to get hold of her daughter's father.

Another first. He'd never come to fisticuffs with a man

over a woman. Never. Not even with his brothers. When Mitch had decided he wanted Liz way back when, he'd stepped aside and never interfered. When Connor had expressed an interest in one of his dates, he'd found a reason to go home and leave the two alone—though, funnily enough, neither of them had seen her again. He'd never felt the need to dole out his own personal brand of justice. But the desire to have his knuckles cleanly connect with the faces of the men who had done Michelle wrong was nearly overwhelming.

He wanted to tell Michelle not to worry, that he'd help her find her daughter. Then it hit him that he didn't have that kind of power. Not in his job. Not over his own damn sense of right and wrong. And what he was doing was definitely beginning to cross the line over to wrong.

He sighed. This morning, Michelle's case had been passed on to Edgar Mollens. Even now, Edgar was likely studying maps, visiting the motel where she'd been staying, checking the phone records for the room and any messages that might have been left for her. If the PI had called her, Edgar would know about it.

Not only were his actions quickly surging toward the wrong column, but one of his colleagues was probably on his tail as he was doing it.

What was he thinking?

Something touched his thigh, and he nearly jumped. He looked down to find Michelle's small hand resting against his slacks, her gaze curious and concerned as she gazed at him.

He knew what he was thinking. He was thinking that Michelle Lambert was a woman, a mother, looking for her child. And he would be a cad if he didn't help her out at least this much.

He turned to the road. Anyway, Ohio wasn't that much

out of their way. What was a few more hours before he took her back to D.C.? Nothing to him. But it could mean the world to Michelle…and to little Lili.

He reached down and covered her cooler hand with his, telling his hormones to take a break and purposefully ending the argument he was having with his conscience.

6

"Is this it?"

Jake squinted through the midday sun at the new, trilevel brick house across the street from where they were parked.

"Yes. Yes, this is it." Michelle stuffed the piece of paper she held and the map into his glove compartment, then reached for the door handle.

"Whoa, whoa, where are you going so fast?"

She blinked at him. "To get my daughter, of course."

"Just like that?"

Energy seemed to emanate from her. "What would you have me do?"

"Wait for a few minutes. Maybe scope the place out first. See if you can see any signs of Lili before you go barging in there."

Her gaze dropped to his mouth and lingered there. "Say it again."

Her request caught him up short. Jake swallowed hard, wondering what he had said to make her momentarily forget her mission and stare at him so provocatively. "Say what?" he fairly croaked.

"My daughter's name."

Jake wanted to refuse, then realized how stupid that would be. "Lili," he said, trying to sound matter of fact, though the name came out as soft as a sigh.

"I like the way you say it." She reached for the door handle again. "I'll only be a minute."

Just like that? One second she was eyeing his mouth like she wanted to devour it, the next she was getting out of the car, hell-bent on getting her daughter back?

Jake started to shake his head, then realized she was going up there alone.

"Hey," he said, getting out of the car. "Wait for me."

"No, no. You'll only confuse Lili." What went without saying took form in the shadow that passed over her features— *if Lili was there.* "Please. Wait there."

Jake reluctantly did as she asked. He settled himself behind the steering wheel and closed the door. Only then did a whole new emotion hit him: fear.

He and kids...well, they didn't really get along. He supposed it might have to do with his size, or that as an adult he hadn't spent a great deal of time around children. But on the few occasions when he'd made the effort, the kids had practically gone off running in the other direction. His brother Marc had caught one of the exchanges at the Manchester County Fair one year and dubbed him Jake Von Frankenstein. Jake had not been amused.

Speaking of brothers, David was probably not very amused right now, either. Checking through his pockets, he found and pulled out his cell phone and punched in the number. The line began to ring while he watched Michelle's tiny but firm behind as she walked up the curved drive of Lili's grandparents' house. Nice suburban place. Just around the back, he caught a glimpse of what looked like one of those wood play centers for kids.

Four rings at the McCoy place and David had yet to pick up. Pops would be in D.C. working. Mitch would be doing something or other around his new horse-breeding operation. He didn't have a clue where his sister-in-law Liz would be. At the diner maybe? Or at the office Mitch had built for her in the barn? They hadn't yet had a phone installed there.

A car passed to his left. Normally, it wouldn't have warranted his attention, except that it slowed. And it was also an exact replica of the one he sat in.

His co-worker, agent Edgar Mollens had tracked Michelle down faster than he'd expected.

Dread, thick and gritty, lined his stomach.

MICHELLE RUBBED her damp palms on her slacks for a third time. She glanced at the large double doors, then at Jake's car, wishing she hadn't asked him to stay behind. Just having him near did wonders for her peace of mind. And if there was one thing she needed right now, it was peace.

Questions, one right after another, swept through her mind. What if the PI had given her a bogus address, just looking for a way to get her out of his office? What if the people who lived here didn't even know Gerald or Lili and called the cops? What if no one was home? Would Jake head for D.C.?

What if she never saw Lili again?

Her heart clogging her throat, she watched her hand rap on the door without any conscious knowledge of having sent the order to her tightly coiled muscles.

Please, please, please…

A full minute later she heard footsteps on tile then a hand touch the doorknob. She realized the occupant must be looking through the peephole. She squared her shoulders and fought the desire to duck to the right. If Lili was there, then Michelle would be the last person Gerald's parents would want to see.

Another minute passed. Michelle's heart beat so loudly, she barely made out a second pair of footsteps on the other side of the door. Finally, it opened.

She stared at the neat, fiftyish woman eyeing her openly. She was wearing a navy and gold silk jogging suit and looked as if she'd just come from the beauty parlor. She resembled any one of the hundreds of older, wealthy tourists that crammed Paris streets in the summer.

This was usually the point where the PI had done the talking. Michelle didn't know how much she'd counted on his presence to break the ice, ask the questions until now. Through Kansas and North Carolina, he'd taken the lead. Now she was on her own.

"Yes? Can I help you?" the woman asked. She gripped the edge of the door with her pink-neon-tipped fingers as if prepared to close it quickly.

Michelle cleared her throat and forced herself to speak loudly enough to be heard. "Yes...hello. I'm Michelle Lambert."

She searched for any sign that the woman recognized her name. There was none.

"Are you Mrs. Evans?"

"Why, yes, I am." The fingers tightened. "Should I know you, Ms. Lambert?"

"I'm looking for my daughter," Michelle blurted.

The door started to close. "I'm not sure I understand."

"Your son...his name is Gerald, yes?"

"Why, yes, it is."

"Is he here?"

"Ms. Lambert, I'm not entirely sure why, but this conversation is making me uncomfortable. Do you mind explaining what it is exactly that you want?"

A man stepped beside Mrs. Evans, and Michelle caught her breath. The resemblance between Gerald and this man was uncanny. She caught a glimpse of exactly what Gerald would look like in twenty or so years. Thinning blond hair, capped teeth, skin the texture of leather from one too many rounds of golf. "Miss, is there something I can help you with?" he asked gruffly. Even his voice was the same.

Michelle opened her mouth, but no sound came out.

The woman looked at the man. "Leland, I can't say as I like this—"

"My daughter, Lili...Elizabeth." Her accent grew heavier, and she fought to enunciate each word clearly. "Do you know where she is?"

The couple looked at each other again, then the man stepped forward, smoothly moving his wife from in front of the door. "The name isn't familiar...Ms. Lambert, isn't it? Neither my wife nor I know anyone with the name Lili. Sorry. Now if you'll excuse us—"

He began closing the door.

"No!" Michelle tried to stop the forward movement.

Footfalls sounded from the sidewalk behind her. Desperately she turned toward Jake. "Please! You must stop—"

Her words died in her throat. Jake wasn't the one behind her. Rather, a man in his mid-forties with dark hair and wearing a pea-green polyester suit stared at her as he pulled something from his jacket pocket. "Ms. Lambert, I'm Immigration Agent Edgar Mollens. I am officially taking you into custody for immediate deportation for the violation of the terms of your visa."

JAKE SCRAMBLED from the car, reflexively reaching for his ID as he strode up the curved drive. Damn, he didn't have his ID. Not that it mattered; Edgar knew who he was. What he should be more concerned with was what Edgar would do once he knew what *he'd* done. Strangely, though, he couldn't bring himself to care. All he knew was an overwhelming desire to protect Michelle from Edgar, who would send her back.

"Let me go, you imbecile." Michelle shouted, tugging her arm from Edgar's grip. "I'm not going anywhere until I get Lili."

Jake came to a stop behind his fellow agent and planted his feet shoulder-width apart. It was all he could do to keep his hands fisted at his sides. What he'd rather do was yank Mollens back by his collar. "Let her go, Edgar," he said evenly.

The agent swung around quickly, his right hand reaching inside his jacket pocket. Jake gave in to the urge to grab him, to prevent him from pulling out the weapon he was surely reaching for.

"Jake."

Edgar settled down and dropped his hands to his sides, a loud sigh indicating his relief. Jake released him, thinking he'd feel better if he had his own firearm. It had taken some effort to leave it in its case yesterday morning. After all, a gun might have come in handy on a hiking trip. A nine millimeter was known to stop all sorts of wild animals.

Jake couldn't say he either liked or disliked the man in front of him. They'd been sent out on a few of the tougher cases together, where backup was required. While he'd disapproved of some of Edgar's personal grooming habits and preferred not to take meals with him, Edgar had scored high on the professional scale. He took his job seriously.

Perhaps too seriously.

He grimaced. *Too* was not a word he would have linked with *seriously* twenty-four hours ago. After all, how could a man be too serious about his job? But standing here looking down the other end of the barrel, so to speak, he gained a perspective he wasn't sure he liked.

Edgar finger-combed the wisps that passed for hair on the top of his head. "Flying monkeys, McCoy, you could have gotten yourself shot. What the hell are you doing here, anyway? Don't tell me. There was a screw-up in D.C. and you were sent out on the same case."

Jake shook his head. "No screw-up."

Edgar's bushy brows drew together. "Then what *are* you doing here?"

"The question is, what are you doing here, Edgar?"

Now that there was no immediate danger, Jake chanced a glance at Michelle. She looked shaken to the bone, her gaze torn between the closed front door and the agent who endangered her freedom to search for Lili. He was filled with a powerful urge to pull her to his side. To block her petite frame from view. To protect her with every ounce of strength he had.

When he returned his attention to Edgar, he found him frowning. "I'm here to deport one Michelle Lambert, illegal alien, back to France." He glanced at Michelle. "Is this her?"

Jake nodded once, curtly.

"Then I'm afraid I have to take her into immediate custody, Jake."

Behind Edgar, he saw Michelle ready to bolt.

The desperate move made his stomach drop down somewhere in the vicinity of his ankles. Where would she go? What could she possibly do? He knew she wouldn't get two feet before Edgar would have cuffs slapped on her wrists.

Edgar's frown deepened. "Are you all right, McCoy? You look a little...odd."

Jake gave a humorless laugh. Odd about covered it. He felt odd. He didn't have a clue what to do with the unfamiliar emotions swirling inside him. He'd always been one to follow his instincts, but they had always led him in the right direction. Now he couldn't be so sure. But he had to follow them anyway.

"You can't take her," he said.

"Okay," Edgar said slowly. "I hear you, Jake."

An image of the ID he'd lost sprinted through his mind, ID he might never see again.

"But you're going to have to give me one good reason why I can't. You know, something for the records."

A reason. Jake searched for one that would stand up to any sort of scrutiny, and somehow he didn't think Edgar would go for the she's-looking-for-her-daughter defense.

His mind finally locked onto one. Without even considering the consequences to his career, he said, "Because she's my wife."

MICHELLE SAT spellbound in the car next to Jake. That agent, Edgar Mollens, motioned for them to drive away first. Jake waved for him to go. Mollens finally drove off, and Jake switched off the engine.

She's my wife.

She didn't know why Jake had said that, but she was mighty glad he had. The agent who had been about to drag her to D.C. had stood in utter shock right along with her for a few moments, then reached out to shake Jake's hand before backing off completely. He'd said something about needing documented proof before the day was out, then got into his car.

She gazed at the man next to her, nearly getting lost in the deep gray of his eyes. She didn't know why he'd done all that he had. Had stopped trying to figure that out since the night before, when instead of driving her to D.C., he'd checked into a motel. Then this morning, did a one-eighty and headed for Ohio. She'd contented herself with being thankful, and thankful only, determined to get the most out of the generous time she could.

Only it appeared that it was all for naught. Yes, the name of the couple in the house across the street may be Evans, but she had no reason to think they knew more than what they had said.

Still, if she had to be taken to D.C., she'd rather Jake do it.

Spending any time at all with Edgar Mollens made her insides go cold.

"Why did you do that? I mean—" She caught herself up short, not wanting to push the issue, not wanting to give him an opportunity to change his mind. But she had to know. "Why did you say I was your wife?"

Jake's expression was somber as he probed her face. "I figured it was the only way to get Edgar to take a hike." A hint of a smile played around his mouth. "Hey, there's something to be said for flying straight your entire life. People have a tendency to believe you when you say something."

"Do you think so? Seemed to me you could have knocked Mollens over with a feather."

"I said he believed me, I didn't say he wasn't shocked. That's one of the drawbacks of being predictable." He trained his gaze out the window. She noted the lines of worry drawn between his brows and felt the incredible urge to reach out and smooth them away. A short time ago, he'd said he was doing what he was because he was at no risk so long as no one knew. What happened now that someone did know? Not only someone, but a man he worked with?

She wrapped her arms around herself.

"What did they say?" he asked.

Michelle blinked at him. "Pardon me?"

He gestured toward the large house. "Are they Gerald's parents?"

She nodded.

"And Lili?"

Michelle stared at where she twisted her hands in her lap. "They say they've never heard of me...or her."

He reached for the door handle. "I'll be right back."

For the second time in as many minutes, Michelle sat dumbstruck as Jake strode toward the Evanses' door. Finally gathering her wits, she clambered out after him, catching up as the door opened to reveal Gerald's father.

Jake reached in his jacket pocket, then grimaced and reached into another. He held out a business card exactly like the one he'd given her. "I'm Agent Jake McCoy. I need your son Gerald's most recent address."

The man had to look up to directly address Jake's gaze. "You didn't say which agency you're with, Agent McCoy."

"No, I didn't. It's on the card, sir." Jake met and held his gaze. "The address, Mr. Evans."

Michelle watched in amazement as the older man gave it to him. Relief threatened to sweep her knees right out from underneath her.

7

JAKE'S HEART pounded in his chest. He tried to tell himself it was because the mere idea of being married, much less to the sexy woman next to him in the car, was terrifying. Then thoughts of night after night in her arms—between her thighs, hearing her soft cries in French—intruded, and he nearly groaned out loud. It didn't matter that any long-term relationship was an improbability. No, an impossibility. His body seemed to have other ideas, and every time he looked at her, trembling from her hair to her feet, he got harder than any man had a right to.

Michelle clutched the piece of paper holding the address for one Gerald Evans in northwest Ohio. "I can't believe this is happening. I don't know what to say...." Her words drifted off, though her lips kept moving.

He'd be willing to bet that her inability to speak was new to her. Chalk up another first.

He couldn't help his foolish grin. Despite the mess he'd just made out of his life with those four simple words back there, "because she's my wife," when Michelle looked at him this way—her eyes liquid milk chocolate, her face practically beaming—he felt a hundred feet tall.

It reminded him of the way he'd felt the first day on the job as an INS agent. He'd been assigned to apprehend an Asian arms dealer who happened to have a taste for a specially ordered type of Chinese herb. He put the only place that sold the herb in New York under surveillance and apprehended the guy. Then he'd watched him go through deportation proceedings and put him on an airplane bound for Peking and the authorities there. It had been one of the most defining moments of his life. He'd felt like he was making a difference, that what he'd accomplished that day not only kept guns off the streets, but told him what he had been put on this earth to do.

What he felt now was a lot like that, only more intense somehow.

"Thank-you should do the trick," he suggested, not sure where the light remark had come from, but glad it had come.

He was rewarded with her smile. "A joke. You just made a joke."

He drove unhindered toward northwest Ohio, toward the address in Toledo where Gerald Evans lived. Two and a half hours, the toll guard had told him. "Yeah. I guess I did, didn't I?"

Michelle slid her hand over his where it rested on the steering wheel. He spread his fingers, and she thread hers through. He gave a tight squeeze. "Thank you," she murmured, her accent thick.

He glanced to find one-hundred-percent pure gratitude lighting her smile. "You're, um, welcome."

She shifted until she was sitting flush next to him, her hip against his, her arm against his side. She sat like that for a long time without saying anything, then slipped her hand from his grip and laid it against his thigh. "Why?" she asked. "I mean, why are you doing all this for me, Jake McCoy? We've, um, already established that it isn't about sex. Anyway, no one's *that* good." Her tiny smile softened her words. "Then you said it was all right so long as no one knew about it, which after what happened at the Evanses' is no longer the case. So...why? Why are you risking so much to help me?"

That was a question he didn't want to examine too closely. He considered telling her it was because it made him feel good, only that had come after he'd done what he had.

He wasn't exactly sure why. One minute he'd been in a pissing contest with Edgar Mollens over who was going to win Michelle's company, the next he was telling his fellow agent he was married to what was now a deportable illegal alien.

"I wanted to give you this chance to find your daughter," he said. Well, it was part of the reason, so he wasn't exactly lying. He just wasn't telling the complete truth, either, though what that truth was, he couldn't say.

She rested her temple against his shoulder. Her gaze caressed him as thoroughly as a touch. "Why?"

He swallowed hard. "I don't know."

Then, suddenly, he did know. He understood all too clearly why it was he was helping this mother find her daughter. What was more puzzling was that he wanted to tell her. He'd never been much for words. He'd learned early on that an expression, a carefully directed look, could accomplish more than any words. And he'd never felt a need to verbally express himself, at least not to the extent that others did.

"I...I was raised without my mother," he said quietly, surprised at the ease with which the words flowed. "She, um, died when I was seven years old." It seemed all his life he had avoided speaking the words aloud, as if afraid openly acknowledging what had been a very tragic point in his life would bring back all the pain. Instead, he felt as if an indescribable weight was shifting in his chest. "I know what it means to grow up without a parent. In my case, it was unavoidable. I couldn't exactly go out and find my mother." He glanced at her, finding her expression warm and curious. "In yours... Well, let's just say that sometime this morning I realized I couldn't take you back to D.C. and put you on a plane without first giving you an opportunity to find Lili." His voice dropped to a near murmur. "A little girl, especially, needs her mother."

She turned, and the look she gave him was direct, so poignant, he felt the strange sensation that she was able to see right through his exterior to what dwelled deep inside.

"So do little boys."

She spoke so quietly, Jake couldn't be sure if she'd said the words or if his subconscious had whispered them.

The first rule he'd learned after his mother's death was that he could never let anyone know how much he mourned her loss. Well, anyone else, anyway. After the funeral, still dressed in their new suits, Pops had dropped him and Connor off at school. He hadn't understood why at the time, but had since assumed that Sean thought it important for them to get back to a sense of normalcy as soon as possible. Only nothing had been normal. And when a bully two years his senior had made it his mission to get dirt on his suit during recess and Jake had found himself pinned to the ground under the older boy's weight, he'd repeatedly cried out for his mother in an agonized way that still echoed through his mind.

He didn't talk to his father for what seemed like weeks afterward. In fact, he rarely spoke to anyone at all. Speaking meant revealing, and revealing meant being stripped of all but his most fundamental defenses.

He realized the car was silent and looked at Michelle. Her brown eyes were moist, as though she'd seen what he'd been thinking. Understood his anguish better than anyone else ever could.

He cleared the emotion clogging his throat. "It was...a long time ago. It's okay. I've adjusted."

"I'm sorry. When I asked you why, I didn't mean to

dredge up anything so painful. I guess I've spent too much time around my daughter. Sometimes it seems every other word out of her mouth is *pourquoi*—sorry, why."

Jake thought of the woman next to him and mentally compared her to what he remembered about his mother. He couldn't say whether they were similar, except for the warm smile Michelle wore whenever she spoke of Lili. That look was intensely familiar. If there was one physical thing he remembered clearly, it was his mother's smile. The tremendous emotional impact of her absence was another. A sometimes tangible shadow against his soul. Always there inside him...at least, until now.

Michelle absently traced a circle of heat on his thigh with her fingers. It was all he could do not to scoot farther down so the circle would be encompassing a completely different area indeed.

"Do you know any French?" she asked.

Jake's semiaroused state went up a notch. He found he liked her speaking in French, perhaps a little too much. But now was not the time to ask her to say something in it, not if he hoped to stay on the road. "A bit."

"What? What do you know?"

He'd never used his limited knowledge of foreign languages for conversational purposes and he felt awkward about doing it now. "Okay. *Je m'appelle* Jake McCoy. Agent Jake McCoy. *Votre passeport, s'il vous plait. Par ici, s'il vous plait.*"

Michelle didn't say anything for a long moment, then the hand disappeared from his thigh; her warmth vanished from his side. She moved to the passenger's seat. He didn't think it possible for two people to be in the same car yet be so far apart. The immediate change in temperature made him want to groan.

"What? What is it? Did I mispronounce something?"

She shook her head, keeping her gaze trained out the window. "No. Your pronunciation was good. Very good." Her voice dropped to a whisper. "Too good."

Then it hit him. In French he'd introduced himself as an agent, asked for her passport, then told her to come with him. Cripes, if anything could have underscored the seriousness of their current situation, that did. How stupid could he get?

He cleared his throat. "What other things does Lili say?"

For a long moment, Michelle didn't move, just sat staring out the window. Then her quiet voice filled the interior of the car like a welcome hum. "She's always asking how old she is."

She fell silent again. Well, that attempt at getting things back on an even keel had certainly worked, hadn't it? If his questions would get only one-sentence responses, then this was going to be one hell of a long ride to Toledo.

He chanced a glance in her direction. Rather than finding her sitting stoically ignoring him, she was fingering something she'd taken from inside her backpack, a faraway look on her face. "She was always disappointed when I told her she was the same age today as she had been yesterday, as if she'd expected to have grown at least five years older overnight." Her short-nailed fingers plucked at the elephant's droopy trunk. "She's growing up so fast as it is. Seems like just yesterday she was this toothless imp who cooed at me when she was happy or shrieked at me when she wanted something. It scares me sometimes, her impatience to grow up so quickly, you know?"

She looked at him then. And Jake's stomach did a double dip. The fear she spoke of was there, along with the undeniable fear of never seeing her daughter again.

She tugged her gaze away. "Ironic, really, that after I invested so much time in pointing out the exact date of her birthday she would spend that day away from me."

Jake felt the sudden urge to wrap his fingers around something—more specifically, Gerald's neck.

Michelle had said Lili's birthday was on Saturday, four days away. Maybe she'd see her daughter by then.

"Is she talking much yet?" he asked, then cringed. Of course she was talking much. Just went to show how little he knew about children.

Michelle's bark of laughter eased some of his tension. "Talking? She's a little speechmaker who's motto is 'have soapbox, will travel.' I don't know what they're teaching her in nursery school, or how she remembers everything so clearly, but when I pick her up, I get lectures on the importance of buckling my safety belt or the significance of brushing my teeth. Then there are the lessons on how she—and I—shouldn't talk to strangers. That was a big lesson, that one. She memorized our phone number. I'm very proud of her, even if half the time she transposes the last two digits. Just yesterday she was telling me about strangers—"

She abruptly halted. Jake's chest tightened at the stricken look on her face. "What? What's the matter?" he asked, wanting to reach for her hand, but unable to. He cursed at his hesitation.

"I...I just said she told me yesterday." Michelle caught her bottom lip between her teeth and shook her head. "Thank you."

Jake grimaced. "Why should you be thanking me?"

Her smile was weak and watery but inexplicably powerful. "For a second there, talking to you made me forget that I haven't seen my daughter for eight weeks. I used the present tense when talking about her, rather than the past. I...I haven't felt this close to her in a long, long time."

This time Jake did reach out, before he had a chance to

think about it, before he had a chance to hesitate. He cupped her cheek, marveling at the way she instinctively leaned into his touch. He rubbed the pad of his thumb against the dampness of her tears. What she had shared about Lili made the mental picture of her come to life. He could see the blond little girl's mouth going a mile a minute, her expressive face contorting as she realized this fact or that. He could see the fire in the woman next to him residing in Lili.

Jake's gaze was drawn to Michelle's provocative mouth. He'd have given anything to kiss her right then, to taste the salt of her tears, the depth of her anguish.

Instead, he forced his gaze to the road before he ran off it.

AS THE CAR cruised along the I-280 bridge over the Maumee River into Toledo, Michelle stared at the city's landscape, her heart pulsing in her chest. She knew an instant of fear. The city was larger than she expected. She'd assumed it would be a smaller town, like so many she'd seen over the past six weeks in her search for her daughter. Like Canton, where Gerald's parents lived. This city was too large, had too many places where one could hide a four-year-old girl.

"Holy Toledo," Jake murmured next to her.

She glanced at him.

He gave her a small smile. "It's just something Klinger used to say on M.A.S.H. You know, Jamie Farr..." His words drifted off, and he turned to the road. "Sorry. It was an American TV show. It may have played in France?"

She shook her head. "I've never watched much television."

"Oh."

She looked down to find herself clutching her backpack for dear life. She forced herself to relax her grip. "Not much farther now."

"Nope," Jake quietly agreed.

"In a few minutes I'll either have Lili back in my arms, or..."

He reached for her hand, and she gladly gave it to him, familiar with the burst of desire that crept up her skin at his every touch. "We'll deal with the other when—if we come to it, okay?"

She nodded. "Okay."

She glanced at him, memorizing the lines of his profile, the strong jut of his jaw, and envisioned what he must have looked like as a little boy—tall, gangly, probably awkward. And silent, always silent.

There was an intensity about Jake McCoy that both intrigued and scared her. She knew what it was costing him to do this for her—on an emotional as well as a career level. Not that he'd ever really tell her. She got the impression that when he made up his mind about something, he did it. No long explanations. No voicing of possible regrets down the line. His reaction to their lovemaking told her that.

Before she knew it, he'd parked at a curb. A sign a couple of blocks back had announced the neighborhood as the Old West End. Large houses towered over nicely manicured streets. The leaves of some of the larger trees were beginning to turn vibrant oranges and reds. Such a pretty place. Such a dark mission.

She turned toward Jake to find him staring at his rearview mirror. She glanced through the back window, half hoping, half fearing she would find him looking at Gerald. Instead, she saw a car resembling the one they were in parking a block down.

He looked at her. "Are you ready?"

She nodded, completely incapable of speech at that moment.

He climbed from the car, and she followed, meeting him on the brick walkway leading to the large Victorian-style home bearing the address Mr. and Mrs. Evans had given them. Michelle knew a stab of sorrow. Gerald had obviously reached a point where money was of no concern to him, yet he'd never offered any kind of financial support. And she didn't want any, she firmly told herself. His ability to inflict such irreversible pain on Lili by ripping her from everything that was familiar, all that she'd ever known, told her that no amount of money could make up for Gerald Evans's crime.

Jake paused at the multipaned wood door, studying her face. Then he gave a quick nod and rang the doorbell. Michelle's heart nearly stopped right then and there.

Nothing. No sound other than the bell reverberating through the large interior.

He rang the bell again.

"Hello, there!" a female voice called.

Jake tugged his gaze from Michelle and sought the woman working on the lawn next door. She wore flowered Capri pants and a plain yellow T-shirt.

"The Evanses aren't home. Susan has gone to visit her parents in Lansing."

"And Gerald?" Jake asked, sounding amazingly like someone familiar with Lili's father.

"He's on a business trip. California, I think. Due back either late tonight or tomorrow." She pulled off her flowered canvas gloves. "Would you like me to tell him you stopped by?"

"No. No, thank you. We were just in the neighborhood and thought we'd drop in. I'll catch him at..."

Michelle leaned closer and linked her hand with his. "Racquetball. He plays racquetball."

"At the club," Jake finished.

The woman nodded and returned to her gardening.

Jake lead the way to the car at a leisurely pace. Michelle had to fight from clinging to his side, to keep her strides reg-

ular. She looked up to find him staring again at the car that
had parked a block up. It was then she realized the driver
hadn't gone into one of the houses. Rather, he sat in the
driver's seat staring at them.

Edgar Mollens.

8

DAMN. Edgar was on their tail, and probably had been since they'd left Canton, Ohio. By now he'd have contacted the main office and have an all-out search going for proof of Jake's marriage to Michelle. And the instant Edgar discovered there was none, Jake had no doubt his peer would pull him over and take Michelle from his custody.

Custody. Now that was an odd choice of words. He felt he had as much control over Michelle's physical nearness as he had over the sun's quick slide to the west. He pressed the gas pedal down as he drove toward the tall buildings of downtown Toledo. He felt more like Michelle held him in an odd sort of custody, an indescribable limbo where he didn't know what was going to happen next, but he knew that he didn't want to be anywhere except where he could be involved.

An idea that had been playing along the fringes of his thoughts since Canton circled, growing closer to the center of his mind—much like the car he drove around Toledo, moving nearer and nearer to downtown.

When all was said and done, the mere concept scared the hell out of him. But it was probably the only option left available to them if they hoped to buy a little more time with Edgar.

He would have to make his fake marriage to Michelle real.

Feeling ill, Jake looked into his rearview mirror. He'd lost Edgar in a snaking trail of traffic, for now. He tightened his hands on the steering wheel and turned a corner, what had to be the county courthouse looming in front of them, a building he'd been keeping an eye out for even before he'd firmly made the decision. Next to him, Michelle had gone silent. He suspected she'd spotted Edgar, as well. Her distance from him was probably better, he argued, despite the itching need to have her smack dab beside him, because given what he was about to do, it was important that his actions not be misconstrued.

Michelle's head turned, not to look at him, but to stare at the courthouse as he pulled into a metered parking space. "What...what are we doing here?"

He switched off the ignition and pocketed the keys. "We're going to get married."

MARRIED?

Michelle stared at him, convinced he had gone completely, utterly nuts.

Sure, she supposed at one point in her life—likely when she was very young and still believed in fairy tales—she had thought marriage romantic. Believed it a union that would bring about a happily-ever-after ending. But with time, she realized there was no pastel-colored world waiting on the other side of the altar. It rained there as surely as it rained here. She'd seen it firsthand, through her parents' marriage, when her mother's death had ruined that happy ending, and her father's second marriage, that ran like a well-organized business powered by convenience and money, rather than thrived as a sacred union through unconditional love.

Then, of course, there was her relationship with Gerald.

All right, as difficult as it was to admit, the morning she'd learned she was pregnant with Lili, she'd idly entertained visions of lacy white dresses, rose-petal-strewn aisles and elaborately iced wedding cakes. But even now she found it odd that she'd never seen her and Gerald forging a life together. Never envisioned them taking Lili on walks through the park. Nor saw him rocking their daughter to sleep in the chair she'd inherited from her mother—the only piece she'd insisted be hers when she'd struck out on her own, no matter what color Jacqueline had painted it. No, just like in the old fairy tales, she had envisioned nothing after the I do part of the ceremony, the cutting of the cake and the opening of the gifts.

Then the marriage proposal had come. Gerald had gotten down on one knee in the middle of the Champs de Mars, held out a ring box to her and asked her to be his wife. And she had looked into his eyes and had seen...nothing. No images of birthdays filled with family and laughter. No Christmases spent together decorating the tree. While their relationship had worked well until that point, it didn't have what it took to take it any further. To have married him...well, to have married him would have been to invite disaster.

So she'd said no. And his obvious relief had only confirmed her thoughts as he'd leaned back on his heels and laughed.

Michelle hadn't realized Jake had rounded the car and stood with her door open until a burst of moist, warm late summer air swept over her. She slowly looked at him, this large, mysterious man who had awakened so much in her, done so much for her. Suddenly she saw wedding dresses and cakes again. She brutally rubbed her eyes to banish the image. And right on the heels of that one she saw Big Jake McCoy standing on a street corner holding Lili's hand in his, waiting for a school bus.

"*Merde.*"

She opened her eyes to find Jake's hand in front of her. "Your presence is required, if this thing is to work," he said.

Michelle sat right where she was, her heart thudding in her chest, her palms slippery and wet.

Jake crouched outside the door, bringing him eye level with her. "There really is no other alternative, Michelle. I think you've figured out that Edgar is on our tail. He's probably waiting right now for proof that we're not married. And the instant he gets it, you can forget about waiting around for Gerald to return later tonight. Edgar wants to see documentation. And it's documentation I have to give him." He glanced toward a couple walking in their direction, the woman dressed in a short white dress holding a tiny bouquet, smiling at the man in the nice suit.

Michelle sank her teeth into her bottom lip, then sighed. "I know."

"You know?" Jake's dark brow rose on his forehead.

She reached out to touch his unshaven cheek. He looked much more real with the stubble on his face, his hair slightly disheveled, his suit a bit wrinkled. "Yes. I know." She smiled. "You are a good man, Jake McCoy. If you promise something, you don't stop until it's done." She rubbed her thumb over the strong planes of his cheek. "And you promised me you would help me find Lili."

His gray eyes darkened to the shade of warm mercury. "This, um, marriage will be in name only, Michelle. You understand that, don't you? If we don't produce a license, Edgar will have you on a plane bound for Paris faster than a flight attendant can say, 'Boarding pass, please.'"

She withdrew her hand and laughed heartily. "Of course I know that. Did you think I intended to make you obey the part about 'until death do us part?'" She shook her head. "This will help you, as well, won't it? I mean, I know you've put your career at great risk by telling that man I was your wife. Producing the proper papers will keep you out of too much trouble, won't it?"

"That's what I'm hoping."

"Good."

His gaze swept her where she sat in the car. "So if we understand each other...why are you hesitating?"

Michelle pretended an interest in her purse, opening it and shuffling through the contents, anything to avoid his direct gaze. "You're going to think this is silly, but..." The couple that had walked by was sitting on a bench under a tree at the side of the courthouse. "I don't know. I think this may be the only time I get married, and...even though it is phony, I at least thought I'd wear white."

Jake skimmed her dark slacks and top, then cast a glance toward the sky and cursed. "Why didn't I think of that?" He glanced at her. "We're going to have to be quick about it. We don't have much time before the license bureau closes. All I can say is it's a good thing we're in Ohio. No residency requirements, no blood test, photo ID is all that's required. Pennsylvania has a three-day waiting period, and you have to have a social security card."

Michelle watched in shock as he closed her door and rounded the car. Within moments they were on the road again. Her heart beat a specific rhythm reserved for this one man who didn't question her foolish, dawdling request, merely acted on it. Within an hour they'd scoured the interior of a local department store and a small florist. Michelle had a white dress and clutched a pretty bouquet of vibrant African violets, and Jake wore a gardenia in his lapel and had two simple rings tucked into one pocket and a disposable camera in another.

As they stood outside the license bureau in the courthouse, license in hand, Michelle was afraid she'd faint flat out.

She glanced at the impossibly tall man standing next to her and smiled. "Jake?"

He looked at her, and she felt that noodle-kneed reaction all over again.

"I just wanted to, you know, say thank you for all this."

His grin was dazzling. "I should be the one thanking you for your quick thinking. Pictures of what looks like a real ceremony will go a long way toward helping us with both Edgar and what will surely be an investigation."

Michelle felt the inexplicable urge to whack him with her violets.

JAKE WASN'T SURE what he'd said, but Michelle had gone from looking like a nervous bride to a woman with murder on her mind within a blink of an eye. He grimaced and looked around the airy courthouse.

Lord, but she looked better than anybody had a right to. He never thought he'd be one to go for the skintight look. In fact, it wasn't all that long ago that he'd openly frowned on such sexy attire. Perhaps it was knowing intimately the treasures clearly outlined beneath the thin, stretchy fabric of Michelle's dress that made him unable to take his eyes off her. He'd be damned if he didn't want to steal her away to some broom closet or supply room and slide his fingers up the hem of that clingy dress and peel her panties down her legs to probe the soft, slick flesh there.

He fought the desire to loosen his tie and led her away from the license bureau door before he overheated.

"So is that it? Are we married?" Michelle asked, following him outside where he dragged in a deep breath.

Jake took in her stricken expression, and an odd tightness gripped his stomach. "No. We, um, have to have someone perform the ceremony, like a judge. No, no, not a judge..."

Around them the lush green of the courthouse lawn looked unnaturally vivid in the afternoon sunlight. Trees dotted the landscape, and curving walkways led to the three other entrances to the stone, domed, four-square building. He caught sight of the couple who had been standing before them in line. Poised in the shade of a tree—the bride in a yellow smock unable to hide that she was well into her third trimester of pregnancy—they were being married by a pastor.

Jake craned his neck to get a closer look at the man of the cloth. His salt-and-pepper hair said he was well into his prime, but his wrinkled, ruddy features made him look far older. He turned slightly away from the couple, opened his timeworn Bible with a flick of a satiny bookmark, then took out a small tin hidden in a cutout hole. He took a quick sip.

Jake nearly burst out laughing.

Michelle backed away from him. "Tell me you're not thinking what I think you're thinking, yes?"

Jake blinked at her. "What?"

"You're not going to ask that...that booze hound to perform the ceremony?"

He grimaced and allowed her to tug her elbow from his grasp. He was struck all over again by how sexy she looked, especially with that pouty frown on her face. "Why not?"

She shifted several times on her towering white heels. "It wouldn't be legal, would it? I mean, the guy can hardly read."

Jake glanced over to catch the old pastor hiccuping. He placed a hand over his mouth and apologized to the young couple, who had eyes only for each other. "Trust me, it's legal enough. Besides, I think it will be fun."

Michelle turned from him, searching the lawn as though another option would pop up at any moment. "There must be someone else."

"We don't have time to find anyone else, Michelle. We've wasted enough time shopping—" He was stopped abruptly by that murderous look in her eyes again. "I know this doesn't look very good, but the sooner we're done with this, the sooner we're back on the road. In the long run, that's all that matters, isn't it?"

The sound of approaching footsteps on the cement walkway pulled Jake's gaze from Michelle. The pastor had finished marrying the other couple and had spotted them. But it wasn't him Jake was concerned about. It was the sight of Edgar bearing down on them from the opposite direction.

"Hidey ho, lovebirds!" the pastor called, fingering his Bible. "Are you looking to get married today?"

"No," Jake said.

At the same time Michelle said, "Yes."

The pastor chuckled. "Seems to me someone's suffering from a mighty case of cold feet."

Michelle stared at Jake, but he didn't have time to explain. Edgar moved closer by the moment. Jake nearly pulled Michelle off those heels as he towed her toward the courthouse, the pastor following right after them.

SAFELY INSTALLED in a judge's outer chambers, Michelle looked at their witness, the drunken pastor, and smiled, hoping the old man would make it through the ceremony still standing. She turned toward the female judge, who was asking her and Jake to join hands.

She was struck once again by how large and strong his hands looked, then noticed how damp they were. Her gaze flicked to his face. While the pastor looked ready to fall over, Jake appeared ready to bolt.

Her smile widened. So big Jake McCoy was afraid of something—namely, matrimony.

Now she understood his desire to be wed by the elderly pastor. The exchanging of vows would have seemed like something out of an American cartoon rather than the real thing. She had convinced him that a judge was the way to go by reminding him that a judge's signature on their wedding certificate would look far better than the pastor's. Practical Jake would never be able to argue that point. Then he'd told her Edgar was in the building.

"Now repeat after me," the female judge said, eyeing them both openly.

Michelle recited the vows carefully, noticing the way Jake avoided her gaze. She resisted the urge to dig her heel into his foot and instead jerked on his hands, forcing him to look at her. She smiled. He turned a frightening shade of green.

Next came Jake's part. Before following the judge's lead, he cast a forlorn look in the pastor's direction. The pastor had other priorities, though. Turning away from the clerk standing nearby, he opened his Bible and took another hefty swig from the tin. Jake grimaced and solemnly repeated after the judge.

How in the hell did I ever get into this mess? he wondered as he recited his vows.

Jake couldn't exactly define what it was he was feeling. He, more than anyone, knew this was all pretend. The dress Michelle had on, the bouquet she held, the rings he was even now fumbling to get out of his pocket, all of it was show, to prove to Edgar and his superiors at the INS that they were married.

Then why did he bear all the hallmark signs of a man who had stuck his head into a guillotine? Marc had looked like he was going to toss his cookies when he'd married Melanie two months ago. Then again, the thought of facing Mel's tight-lipped mother, Wilhemenia Weber, across a dinner table at holidays... Jake cringed. Hell, that would be enough to make any man think twice.

And then there was Mitch. He could just imagine what had gone through Mitch's mind when his bride was late for the ceremony...again. At least this time Liz Braden had eventually shown up, unlike seven years ago when Jake had silently nursed Mitch back from a subsequent week-long drinking binge that had left them all the worse for wear.

The clerk snapped their picture in front of the judge. Jake winced. His hands shook as he opened the box that held both rings. He took out the smaller of the two simple gold bands. The smile Michelle gave him as she held out her hand nearly knocked him over. He'd noticed how tiny her hands were before, but now, with one lying against his palm, it looked downright childlike. He touched the ring to the tip of her ring finger, then nearly dropped the blasted thing. He slowly budged it up her finger, sunlight glinting off the narrow band. The clerk snapped another picture.

Michelle held her other hand out. He blinked at it, then at her. "Oh." He fumbled for the box again, then handed the other ring to her.

He gritted his teeth, wondering how he'd let her talk him into buying two bands. Sure, they'd been on sale, two for one, of all things. But all they'd needed was the one. His thoughts seemed to manifest themselves in body reaction. Though the band had slid on easily at the store, Michelle now had to twist and turn it to force it up his finger. It was all he could do not to stop her and toss the thing out the open window.

He knew the instant the ring hit home at the base of his finger. He felt a weird sort of heat, as if she'd fused the sucker there. He stared at the symbolic piece of jewelry and nearly hurled.

"You can now kiss the bride," the judge said with a smile.

He stared at the woman. Was she insane? Kiss the bride? The last thing he felt like doing was kissing....

Michelle's silky soft lips met with his. His gaze was riveted to her face as she stood on tiptoe to slant her mouth against his. Everything he was coming to know as her surrounded him: her sweet smell, her lush body, her soft hair.

He groaned and threaded his fingers through the curly hair over her ears, holding her still so he could kiss her more deeply. The heat that began with the ring steamed toward his groin. God, but this woman tasted better than any one woman had a right to—warm, inviting, downright sexy.

The clerk cleared her throat. Jake pulled away, half dazed, and looked toward the sound just as the flash of the camera went off again.

9

MICHELLE PRACTICALLY had to jerk him from the judge's chambers after the picture-taking and the paper-signing, for all the control he seemed to have over his body, much less the situation. But as determined and wiry as she was, she was no match for his shear size. Ten feet down the hall, she gave up and instead pressed him against the cool wall.

Jake blinked at the decidedly wicked smile she gave before slanting her mouth against his and boldly running her tongue across his lips.

"What was that for?" He practically croaked the words afterward.

She shrugged lightly. "You looked like you needed it."

His grin originated in his chest. "Boy, do you ever have that right."

He brought his mouth down on hers.

Ah, if anything could have taken his mind off the past thirty minutes, this was it. He leaned against the wall and hauled her against him. Despite the difference in their sizes, they fit amazingly well together, her mouth on his, his growing erection pressing against the soft flesh of her lower belly. He launched a full-scale assault on her mouth, marveling at the textures there, the smoothness of her teeth, the rasp of her tongue as she gave as good as she got. He pressed his hands harder against the small of her back, drawing her closer still as she hastily undid the top few buttons of his shirt. He shuddered as she pressed the heat of her palms against the bare skin of his chest.

"There," she said, kissing him again and giving his tie a yank. "That's much better."

The sound of approaching footsteps sent reality crashing in on him. What was he thinking? They were in the middle of a county courthouse, for cripe's sake. He dragged his mouth from hers, then closed his eyes and rested his temple against her soft hair, sucking in desperately needed air.

The clearing of a male throat.

Jake grimaced. The pastor must have followed them out, perhaps looking for more compensation than the tenner he'd given him to witness the ceremony. Michelle shifted to look at their company and went stiff in his arms. Jake opened his eyes to stare at Edgar Mollens.

Jake patted his jacket pocket where he'd put the certificate of marriage. He grinned. "Edgar, old buddy, old pal, old friend of mine."

Edgar's fleshy features darkened. "Get off it, McCoy. I knew there was something fishy about this whole thing right from the start. You, married? And to an illegal alien on high alert, at that?" He shook his head. "I knew there was no way in hell. Everyone at the office knows you'd send your own mother back to Kosovo if you found out she was an illegal."

Jake's spine snapped to attention. He reminded himself that his co-worker had no idea his mother had died long ago. Still he couldn't help saying, "My mother's family came over on the *Mayflower*, you idiot."

Edgar's brows budged up on his wrinkled forehead. "So the silent one is capable of anger. I'm sorry to say I've lost a bet."

He folded Michelle's hand in his. "Come on, let's go."

Edgar grabbed her other arm. "You can go wherever you like, McCoy—at least until you're scheduled to appear before the review board back home. This one...well, she goes back with me and is on the first plane out of here."

"Keep pushing it, Edgar, and I'll show you just how angry I can get," Jake said evenly, his blood steaming through his veins and roaring past his ears.

"Are you threatening me?"

Jake had at least six inches on the other agent, and he used them now to his advantage by stepping closer. Edgar hesitated, then stumbled, but didn't release Michelle. "No, I'm *promising* you that if you don't unhand my wife right this minute, I'm going to break your hands."

Edgar's bark of laughter echoed through the hall. The old pastor turned to look at them where he stood near the stairs. "Get off it, Jake. I just had Pauline check every courthouse between here and D.C. You two are about as married as a goose and a dove. That's a *cooked* goose."

Jake calmly placed his hand on Edgar's right shoulder and squeezed until he released his grip on Michelle, then he slipped the marriage certificate from his pocket. He slapped it against the agent's chest. "Here you go, buddy. Read it and weep." He took Michelle's hand again.

"For crying out loud, you haven't seen the last of me, Mc-Coy!" Edgar called after them.

DESPITE what had just transpired at the courthouse, Jake felt as though a Just Married sign complete with tin cans and streamers was posted to the back of his car, for all the giddiness he felt. Which was ridiculous. Because not even an hour ago, he'd been close to passing out dead cold from nerves. And because while he and Michelle were *legally* married, they weren't *really* married. Theirs was a marriage of convenience. Not for money. Not for prestige. But because Michelle needed a way to stay in the country long enough to find her daughter, and he needed to give it to her. No matter what Edgar and his superiors might think.

The sensation had hit him immediately upon leaving the courthouse. After giving Edgar the certificate. After Michelle had kissed him senseless in the hall. And after she had paused outside the door where prospective jurors were waiting to be called, and tossed her small bouquet over her shoulder. All nervousness had left him. And all he could think about, sitting in the car next to her, heading to the area where Gerald Evans lived, was that he wanted his wedding night. Except in this case it would be his wedding evening. Hell, he didn't care what it was, and he didn't care that last night he'd had Michelle every which way but loose. He wanted to explore every sweet inch of her, thrust into her slick, hot flesh, watch the graceful line of her neck as she tossed her head back and made those soft whimpers that drove him absolutely crazy.

He wanted to do it now.

He gripped the steering wheel tightly and took deep, measured breaths. It was either try to get a grip or pull over to the side of the road and have at her. Haul her over so she straddled him in that clingy little dress. Launch an oral assault on her pointy breasts right through the lacy material of her dress. Thrust his fingers up to touch her panties, then immerse them in her dripping wetness.

He shifted to ease the discomfort of his semiaroused state.

Before he went giving himself over to needs he'd never thought he possessed, he had some business to attend to.

He reached across Michelle's lap to the glove compartment. He had just opened it when she touched his arm.

He glanced into her concerned face. "You...that man..." She took a deep breath, her fingers tightening on his arm. "After all this is done, you're going to be in trouble, aren't you?" She bit her bottom lip. "I mean more than just getting fired. You might be put in..."

"Jail?" He finished her sentence for her, his throat closing around the word.

She stared at him, wide-eyed.

"Yes. It may very well come to that. Edgar may have that wedding certificate, but it's only a matter of time before he gets the proper documentation to haul both of us in for intense scrutiny by immigration review...or even court." But he didn't want to think about any of that. No. He wanted to concentrate on what needed to be done and try to accomplish it in whatever time they had left.

He punched two buttons and placed the cell phone to his ear.

Two rings, then he heard, "McCoy Place, David here."

Jake grimaced. Of all the people to answer the phone. "It's Jake."

"For God's sake, man, where in the hell are you? Pops is this close to putting an APB out on your sorry ass. Mitch has been on the horn with some of his old friends at the FBI, and all the provisions I packed for our hike are rotting in my backpack near the door."

Jake slanted a glance at his pack in the back seat. "Good." He cursed under his breath. "Not about the trip. About Mitch's being on the phone with the FBI. Look, I need a favor."

"No, we haven't seen your blasted ID."

"This is not about my ID, David." He realized that he hadn't absently patted his jacket pocket since sometime last night. At the Evanses' in Canton didn't count, because that had been official...well, somewhat official. He glanced to find Michelle watching him in curiosity. "I need to find out when an individual is due to fly into Toledo, Ohio, and on which flight."

"Holy Toledo?" David said.

"Yeah. Can you do that for me?"

"I'll get Mitch on it right away," his brother promised. "I take it I should cancel my plans, then?"

"Plans?" Jake switched ears. What plans did one need to go hiking through the mountains?

"Yeah, for the cabin I rented. I somehow couldn't envision you roughing it in a tent. That's why the food is rotting in my bag. It was supposed to go into the cabin refrigerator sometime last night."

Jake cracked a smile. The youngest McCoy was capable of a few surprises of his own. "Why didn't you put the food in Pops's fridge?"

"Why didn't I put the food in Pops's fridge?" David repeated sardonically. "Hmm, maybe because we've all spent the past twenty-four worrying about you? And I didn't remember the stuff was in there until I pretty much heard that you were okay by your voice? You know, it would have helped if you'd answered your cellular."

"The battery went dead," Jake lied, cringing.

"Yeah, right." David muttered a mild curse. "Look, forget about it. You don't have to apologize, Jake. Or were you going to apologize?"

Jake cleared his throat and cast another glance in Michelle's direction. Lord, she looked good. "Sorry, little bro."

The silence on the other end of the line was deafening.

"David?"

"Hmm? Oh, yeah, I'm here. Just a little shocked, is all. Did you actually just say you were sorry?"

"Moron."

"No, wait, I want to confirm this, because I don't think that in all my thirty years on God's green earth have I ever heard you say that word."

"Yeah, well, you may be hearing a lot of it in the coming days, so get used to it now."

"What? Why?"

"Mitch off his phone yet?" Jake asked.

Heaving a sigh, David said, "Yeah. Hold on a sec, will ya?"

A moment later, Mitch picked up the phone. He'd listened in on David's end of the conversation, so he didn't waste time with small talk. Of all his brothers, Mitch was the one who understood Jake best. He cut straight to the chase, asking for the name of the individual and the airport he was flying into. Jake asked him if Liz had kept any of her credit cards in her maiden name. Without hesitation, Mitch gave him a number along with an expiration date, then agreed to call and make hotel reservations for him at a downtown Toledo hotel Jake had seen while trying to shake Edgar.

After all this was taken care of, there was a short pause. Jake waited for Mitch's questions.

It was not the sort of question he'd expected. For that, among all the other things Mitch was doing for him, Jake was thankful. "You think you're going to be back by Thursday?" Mitch asked.

"I don't know."

"Good enough. You just make sure you call us if you need anything, you hear? I mean anything."

Jake grinned. "Yeah. Thanks, Mitch. Call me back on the cellular when you get the info."

He pressed the disconnect button, then put the phone on the seat between him and Michelle.

Michelle didn't quite know what to make out of the conversation she'd just heard. She felt that in the past two days, she'd come to know Jake quite well. Certainly not every little detail of his life. She'd be the first to admit she didn't know what the guy ate for breakfast, though she suspected it would be something wholesome and fruity. But he had a brother? And what was it he'd said about the FBI? And just who, exactly, did he know who had the type of power to find out which plane Gerald was on?

She sat back and wrapped her arms around herself, feeling somewhat distanced from the man beside her. But that's not what bothered her most. What disturbed her was that she wanted to know everything about him. Not because it applied to their situation, but because it applied to him. That was disturbing indeed.

She absently turned the simple gold wedding band on her finger. "Your brother?"

Jake nodded and scrubbed his face with his hands.

"He's younger than you?"

He looked at her blankly.

"You said little bro, which I'm assuming means little brother?"

"Oh, yeah. That was David, the youngest. There are five of us, all told."

"Five?" Michelle blinked and looked at him from head to toe. There were four men out there somewhere just like the man next to her? Well, probably not *just* like him. But surely they would be similar in some ways, which lead her to wonder which.

He nodded. "There's Connor, the only one older than me. Then Marc, Mitch and David." He gave a lopsided grin. "Shocking, huh?"

"Not shocking, really," she said, lost in thought. "Which one has the connection to the FBI?"

"You heard that, did you?" He flicked on his right blinker and stopped at a red light. "That would be Mitch. He and his new wife have resurrected the old Connor—that's my mother's family name—horse breeding farm, but he used to be with the FBI before he was a PI." He stopped. "Long story. Anyway, if any of the McCoy men can find out which plane Gerald's on, Mitch can."

The McCoy men? The way he said it made them sound like an outlaw gang. Something tingled at the edges of her mind. The Hatfields and McCoys. Weren't they an American legend of some sort? Feuding families?

No, no, the McCoys wouldn't be outlaws, no matter Jake's current circumstances. And now that she knew his brother Mitch was former FBI... She connected the dots of similarity. "Don't tell me. You're all in law enforcement?"

His grin threatened to swallow his handsome face. "Yes. How'd you guess?"

"Even your father?"

"A D.C. police officer. So is David. You didn't answer my question," he pointed out.

It was Michelle's turn to smile. "Call it a lucky guess."

"Anyway, rather than driving around town until Mitch or David gets back to me, I thought we'd check into a hotel, catch something to eat and..."

His words drifted off into a suggestive never-never land that left Michelle hot all over. If only he didn't appear so surprised by his own words. "And?" she prompted.

"And wait until we can go get Lili back."

Michelle's thumb stilled where she played with her ring. *Lili.* Suddenly, inexplicably, she felt pulled into two different directions—and felt instantly guilty for it.

During her time with Jake, she'd felt alive in a way she hadn't for a long, long time. No, alive wasn't the word she was looking for. She felt like a woman. Not someone's mother. Not a great chef. She felt desirable and sexy, and suspected she had merely thrown a stone into a secret well of sensual need deep inside her. And Jake was the willing— well, okay, reluctantly willing—catalyst for that. And finding Lili...

Being reunited with her daughter would end all that.

She bit her bottom lip. Leave it to her to discover the one man who could make her feel like a woman again, only to find that man lived halfway across the world from her. And was an INS agent to boot. What was it her stepmother always said? If there was trouble, she was sure to stumble across it. Or put her foot it in. One or the other.

She agreed with Jacqueline. She was in *really* bad shape.

She looked at the upscale hotel Jake stopped in front of. It wasn't all that far from the courthouse. She'd guessed some time back that he was traveling in ever widening circles around the downtown area. Whether it was to guarantee they weren't being followed or to gather his thoughts, she couldn't be sure. But she'd gotten a full-scale glimpse of the city. Older stone buildings hunkered alongside newer, modern constructions. The Maumee River bisected the city from its east side, all manner of boats—from paddleboats that had been transformed into floating restaurants to small motorboats—docked on the west side of the river, not far from where they were. Next to the hotel, a tower of metal and glass stretched toward the sky, its blue-tinted panes reflecting the sinking sun.

A valet opened the door for her. Michelle looked at Jake, a funny little tickle starting low in her belly.

"Go ahead."

"Are you sure? Wouldn't it be better if we, um, checked into a motel or something closer to Gerald's?"

He tugged at his tie and glanced in the other direction before saying quietly, "I wanted to treat you to something, you know, a little more special. Seeing as it's our honeymoon and all."

Michelle didn't miss the suggestion laced through his words. The mere prospect of having him lave her breasts with his hot, soft tongue, of cradling him between her thighs, was enough to make her catch her breath.

The valet motioned toward a bellboy. "Howard, take this lucky couple's bags inside, won't you? We have newlyweds on board tonight."

Michelle felt her cheeks go hot. She took the young man's hand and climbed out of the car, tugging at the hem of her white dress as she did so. She looked at the elegantly lighted exterior of the hotel, the posh lobby visible through the sliding glass doors, the well-dressed, solicitous staff. She'd stayed in the Paris Ritz once. She'd just graduated from culinary school and was in the mood for a celebration. Wanted to be surrounded by the atmosphere in which she hoped one day to work. But while the surroundings were luxurious, the employees impossibly polite and discreet, she hadn't felt quite the same kind of welcome. And while she'd enjoyed the fine appointments of her room, the thrill had lasted for about five minutes, before loneliness had settled in on her. She'd ordered room service, drank an entire bottle of champagne by herself, then passed out.

This was an entirely different situation, indeed.

She glanced at where Jake spoke to the valet, shivering at his strong profile. For a dangerous second, she allowed herself to believe that she *was* on her honeymoon. That her childhood faceless groom wanted to make sure everything was perfect for their first night together. Then she watched as her simple bag and the backpack and gear on the back seat were loaded onto a cart, and reality pressed in on her from all sides. Still, she wanted to give herself over to the seductive lure of the fantasy, if just for the next hour or so. Until Jake's brother called. Until she could no longer ignore life and reality. She caught herself restlessly caressing her neck and smiled. She and Jake...well, they could fit a lifetime of loving into an hour.

JAKE PLAYED AT trying to give the concierge his credit card, but as he'd instructed, Liz had been emphatic that the charges go on her bill when she called a short time ago. He slid his MasterCard into his wallet, and the overhead light reflected off the bit of gold on his ring finger. His breath froze in his lungs.

Whoa. He was married.

In a strip of mirror behind the desk, he caught a glimpse of Michelle standing behind him looking sexier than ever. He was afraid he'd never draw another normal breath.

"This way, Mr. Braden."

It took a moment for Jake to realize the bellboy had called him by Liz's maiden name. He turned and acknowledged the young man then tucked Michelle's hand into the crook of his arm.

A decided air of expectancy clung to him as they took the river view elevator to the fifth floor. He heard Michelle swallow next to him. All he knew was that if the blasted bellboy wasn't in the enclosure with them, he'd have pressed Michelle against the wall right then and there. Damn, he couldn't breathe. He cleared his throat and ignored the heat that seemed to emanate from Michelle, nearly searing him through his sleeve where her hand rested.

Two more floors. One...

Finally, the doors slid open and the bellboy led the way down the detailed carpeting toward a set of double doors at the end of the hall. The doors were swung inward. He was so relieved that they were going to be alone together, in the privacy of a closed room, he easily swept Michelle into his arms, intoxicated by her surprised gasp, then her nervous laugh. He stepped into the room, barely seeing anything around him. All he could do was gaze at Michelle. Her curly hair was tousled and sexy. Her tongue darted out to moisten very kissable lips. And her eyes had darkened to a seductive shade of whiskey.

Jake turned to slip the bellboy a tip, surprised to find the doors closed, the young man nowhere in sight.

"You know what it means when you carry a bride over the threshold, don't you?" she murmured, pressing her tiny breasts against the wall of his chest.

He realized that's exactly what he'd just done. "Um, no. What does it mean?"

"Good fertility."

Then, suddenly, everything that was Michelle possessed him.

Pulling herself up by her hands around his neck, she claimed his mouth with a hunger and passion that nearly knocked him over backward. He gently slid her down the length of his body until she was standing. He pressed her into his aching erection, thrust his fingers up the back of her dress and cupped her lush little bottom in his hands. She wore no nylons. There was nothing between him and her curved, sweet, hot flesh except her lacy panties. For someone so tiny, she found a way to cradle him just so, making him dizzy with pleasure, urgent with need. Everything around them slipped away. The large room. The river view. The fact that somewhere out there Edgar Mollens was even now trying to figure out a way to get both of them to D.C. and make them the targets of an immediate immigration review. His world narrowed to Michelle Lambert and Michelle Lambert alone.

All at once, he couldn't seem to get enough of her. Her mouth. Her soft flesh. Even as she sought to put distance between them for a moment so she could rip off his jacket, they contorted themselves in order to maintain the connection of their mouths. Oh, and what a great mouth she had, too.

She finally stripped him completely and backed him unceremoniously toward the bed, the soft, needy words in French she murmured driving him wild. He loved it when she spoke French. Down he went. And off went her dress as he pulled it over her head, her pale nipples bare of bra and swaying as she dragged the material down her arms. Jake reached for them, but she grabbed his hands and held them still at his sides.

The first long, lingering flick of her tongue as she dragged it across his abdomen was nearly her last, because he almost lost it right then and there. Around and around, up and down, she dragged her tongue across his skin, watching his reaction until he clamped his eyes closed and gritted his teeth to keep from climaxing prematurely.

Then, abruptly, she was gone.

Jake opened his eyes to find her breasts at eye level. Curving his fingers around a small orb, he hungrily sucked her nipple deep into his mouth, satisfied at her low moan, then pulled the other in, restlessly moving from one to the other until they were wet from his attentions. She worked her thumb between his mouth and her flesh, rubbing the pad along his bottom lip to separate them, then following briefly with her mouth. Then she slid down the length of him, every glorious inch of her stomach rubbing against his straining erection.

He watched in rapt fascination as she slowly, torturously ran her fingertips down his engorged shaft, giving him a thoughtful, thorough squeeze. He thrust his hips upward, impatient to be inside her.

But that evidently wasn't part of her plan. Instead, he nearly came off the bed at the hot feel of her mouth encircling the tip of his erection. If the sensation of her dragging her tongue across his abdomen had been maddening, this...this was downright sinful.

He alternated between clamping his eyes shut and watching her as she slowly slid her lips over the length of him. His hips bucked involuntarily.

She drew away for a moment and shifted to sit at his side, piling her curls on one side of her head as she bent to her task again. Her white lacy panties were plainly visible, as was the springy wedge of her womanhood beneath.

Michelle's mouth went over him again. He fought the need to thrust upward again, and lost. She cupped him, squeezing ever so gently, and instantly the sensation of imminent climax subsided, leaving only the intense heat of her mouth.

Gritting his teeth, he lifted himself on his elbows and reached for her. She gasped as he lifted her, carefully maneuvering until she was pantyless and her knees rested on either side of his head, so that they could enjoy each other simultaneously.

Jake's throat choked off air as he eyed her engorged womanhood mere inches from his chin. He swallowed the saliva gathering in his mouth. He'd never viewed a woman's intimate parts this close before. The fact that Michelle was allowing him such close contact with her spoke volumes.

There was something inherently beautiful about the way her springy dark hair peppered her skin, enough to protect, but not enough to completely shield the area from view. The way the skin swelled on either side of her distended pink, sensitive flesh. He realized there was a reason writers often referred to a woman's private parts as a split ripe peach. Because right now he was filled with an insatiable urge to devour her.

He tentatively fastened his lips around the enlarged, hooded core of her femininity. She instantly threw her head back and cried out, making all the awkwardness more than worth it.

Wow. A greater aphrodisiac he had never known. He

pursed his lips around the tender nub and nibbled, before drawing it into his mouth and swirling his tongue around the tip. If their coming together last night had been all about take, this was all about giving. He wanted to possess Michelle in a way he'd never wanted to possess another woman. He wanted to give her the same type of pleasure she was showing him. He wanted to make her writhe in need, call out his name, cling to him as though her very life depended on it.

The gentle rocking of her hips told him that his inexperience mattered not at all. He tugged his mouth away from her and ran the length of his tongue down her narrow crevice, then thrust it into her tight, hot channel. Instantly, she pulled her mouth away from him and whimpered, her body shuddering in wild abandon, her hips moving in time with his thrusts.

The tips of her breasts teased the muscles of his stomach with her every move. She curled her fingers more tightly around his erection, but while her actions were driving him crazy with desire, he wanted to be inside her *now*.

Grasping her hips, he gently nudged her bottom down his torso until she sat, her back facing him, her hair a sexy, tangled mass around her face as she gazed at him over her shoulder.

Jake admired the long, graceful lines of her back, following her spine with his thumbs until he reached her behind, where he spanned to grasp her hips again. She reached for a condom in the basket on the bedside table, then guided the coated tip of his erection to rest against her slick, hot aperture. He tightened his grasp and thrust upward with every ounce of energy he possessed. Her head snapped back, and she moaned, the sultry, sexy sound winding around him, clutching him as he pulled back and thrust again.

"Oui, oui, mon cherie," she murmured, nearly catapulting him over the edge.

She moved her body in perfect symphony with his until her breathing came in ragged gasps. She leaned forward and rested her hands on the mattress between his legs, her movements becoming slower, more concentrated, her moans deeper. Jake was unable to tear his gaze away from where they were joined. His hard flesh fusing with her soft, her wetness dripping over his erection. He reached down and cupped her bottom in both hands, then spread her a little farther open, allowing for even deeper contact...and completely lost it.

The world exploded into a flash of white hot light.

10

MICHELLE HAD NEVER felt so utterly boneless, sated, exhilarated. She fastened the fluffy white hotel robe around her damp skin as she left Jake behind in the shower, a decidedly wicked-feeling smile claiming her lips. Before their first time together, she'd suspected that Jake was an ingenue when it came to matters of sex...well, not an ingenue, exactly, but very definitely conservative and reserved.

Tonight he'd shown *her* a few things she hadn't thought were possible. Just thinking about it made her want to climb into that huge bed to wait for him so they could start all over again.

For the first time, she glanced around the room. Thick white carpeting, monstrous king-size bed, stylish curtains with matching bedspread, gilt-edged mirrors and antique furniture reproductions all combined to make it comfortable and tasteful. But it was the river view from the window covering one full wall that caught her attention. The setting sun slanted bright orange streaks across the Maumee River. It looked magical....which was fitting, because this evening had certainly proved magical to her. She wrapped her arms around herself, then stared at the thin gold band on her finger. Strange that such a simple piece of metal could signify so much. Not unlike Jake. She'd never thought she was attracted to the strong and silent type. But this one man...he'd slipped inside her heart with the simplest of ease.

God help her, she loved him. In an all-consuming way that

made her want to forget who she was. Forget who he was. Wipe the slate clean and start all over again. Just him, her and Lili.

The muffled chirp of a cell phone filled the room. She glanced first at the bed, then at the pile of clothes on the floor. Bending over, she fished through the items until she found Jake's jacket. She stepped toward the bathroom as she took the slender receiver from a side pocket.

"Jake?" she called into the bathroom.

She was answered by his tuneless humming. She could have sworn the song was *"You Are My Sunshine,"* but she couldn't be sure. She was more concerned with the ringing instrument in her damp palm.

She stepped into the other room, staring at the phone as it continued to ring. It could very well be Jake's brother bearing news of Gerald's return to Toledo. The possibility both frightened and excited her. Excited her because it meant she might very soon be holding little Lili in her arms again. Frightened her because it would mean the abrupt end to all she and Jake had found in each other's arms.

Biting hard on her bottom lip, she pressed the receive button. "Hello?"

"I'm sorry, I must have dialed wrong," a male voice said.

"No, no, wait!" Michelle quickly interjected.

Too late. The line was dead.

Sighing, she pressed disconnect, then sank onto the mattress. She stared at where steam billowed out from the bathroom. Perhaps she should go in there and climb into the shower with Jake. See if there were any spots she missed on the first go-around. And even if there weren't, she could always start again from the top and make her way down that long, lean body—

The phone rang again, and she nearly dropped it.

This time she didn't hesitate. "Hello? Jake McCoy's... phone."

Silence. Then, "Who's this?"

Michelle closed her eyes. Such a simple question. Such a complicated answer. "Michelle," she said, clearing her throat, aware that her accent had thickened with the heightening of her nerves. "You have information on when Gerald Evans is scheduled to return to Toledo, yes?"

Silence again. "Michelle who?"

She tucked her hair behind her ear and closed her eyes. "Lambert. I'm..." What? Jake's wife? Oh, wouldn't that make this conversation interesting? "You're Jake's brother, yes? David? Or Mitch?"

"Mitch. And you're Jake's... I'm sorry, I think I missed the second half of your statement."

"Friend," she said, instead of any of the other dozen answers that flooded her mind, *lover* topping the list. But still, even that title didn't seem to fit. He was much, much more than her lover.

She looked up to find the man in question watching her from the bathroom doorway. Michelle felt her cheeks go hot. "One moment, please, while I put Jake on the line."

He crossed the room, a towel hung low on his slender hips. Michelle swallowed hard, longing to lick the lingering water droplets from the clean skin of his stomach. She slowly held out the cell phone to him. "It's your brother Mitch."

Jake took the phone and grinned at her. "Bet your conversation with him was interesting."

She couldn't help smiling. "Yes. That it was. He hung up on me." At his raised brow, she explained, "The first time. Then he called back." She motioned nervously toward his hand. "He's waiting with news of Gerald now."

When he raised the phone to his ear to receive the information, in a flash, all good humor left her. Michelle pushed from the bed and strode toward the large picture window, her attention more on Jake's reflection in the tinted glass than the lights beginning to come to life on the nearby suspension-cable bridge.

"Mitch," Jake said, making the one word sound like a greeting and a command for him to speak. Michelle noticed his grimace. "Never mind who Michelle is. What have you got?" A pause. "Uh-huh. Ten o'clock. I see. Yeah, yeah, I know. I owe you big for this." Another pause then Jake glanced at her. "No, you haven't met her before. Yeah, I'll tell her." He turned and slowly paced away from her, but she could still make out what he said. "It's complicated. I can't fill you in on all of the details now, but I'm helping Michelle find her daughter, Lili.... Yes, I suspect this Gerald Evans has her. That's all I can tell you now. What?" A deep-throated chuckle. "Yes, she's...attractive." A pause. "Thanks, Mitch. Yes, I'll keep you posted."

He disconnected, then tossed the phone to the bed. "Mitch asked me to apologize for his abruptness."

She shrugged, pretending nonchalance, when in all honesty, nonchalance was the last thing she felt. Only problem was, she was having a difficult time defining exactly what she did feel. Adrift? Uncertain? On the one hand, she longed to be a part of all that was familiar to Jake, wanted his brothers to know who she was and hoped they accepted her. On the other, she knew it was foolish for her to forge anything that stretched beyond now, this moment, because the next moment might not be hers to decide what to do with.

"So," she began, tucking the robe more tightly around her. "Was your brother able to get the information?"

Jake said nothing for a long moment. He sought and found her gaze in the smooth glass and held it. He looked so solemn. All the sexy playfulness that characterized the past two hours slipped away, replaced by the stark reality of now.

She'd known this moment would come. But she couldn't say she'd been fully prepared for it. Her heart beat a steady, almost painful staccato in her chest. The current of electricity that had hummed through her muscles only moments before was replaced by an odd numbness.

Jake finally spoke to her reflection. "Yes. Gerald's plane arrives in an hour." He cleared his throat. "Mitch was also able to verify that Evans booked a companion ticket. Looks like Lili is going to be with him."

ADRENALINE RUSHED through Jake's veins, strong and pure. It had been a long time since he'd felt so driven to do something. It was likely he'd never felt it. He forced himself to concentrate on when that last time would have been, but his mind refused to cooperate. All he could think about was that in the next few minutes, everything he'd come to know in the past two days could change.

He glanced at Michelle, who stared at the front of Gerald Evans's house unblinkingly. He'd have given anything to have left her at the hotel, in that posh honeymoon suite wrapped up in that too large terry robe, somehow managing to look as sexy as all get out when any other woman would have been overwhelmed, lost in all that white. In the shower, he had entertained visions of him saving the day, sweeping little Lili from Gerald's custody then returning to the hotel room to reunite Michelle with her daughter.

But Michelle would have none of it. She'd been charmingly furious when he even started to suggest she stay behind. She'd go without him if need be, she'd told him. And nothing short of tying her up would stop her.

He suppressed the urge to touch the end of a curl that impeded his view of her face, the image of her tied to that soft bed tempting him. It would be a mistake to touch her because he needed to be sharp. Needed to forget notions of tangled sheets and soft moans, hot tongues and even hotter other refuges.

He forced a swallow down his tight throat, then looked in his rearview mirror to see a car approaching.

"I think this is it," he said quietly.

Michelle nearly leaped from the car. Jake gently grasped her arm and held her still.

"We need to see if he has Lili with him first."

She bit her lip and nodded. "Of course. Yes, you're right."

The late-model Lincoln all-terrain vehicle slowed, then pulled into the drive to their left. Yes, it was Gerald, all right. But if he was going to do what he thought...

The garage door began to open.

Jake cursed and opened his door. "Wait here."

He knew the instant the words were out of his mouth that Michelle would disobey them. But he couldn't concern himself with that. If little Lili was in that car, then the garage door would impede them from confirming the fact.

As he hurried up the driveway, the clap clap of Michelle's shoes sounding on the pavement behind him, he patted his chest. He realized he was checking for his ID. Of course, his firearm probably would have been equally welcome right about now.

The Lincoln pulled inside the garage. Jake ducked under the closing door. Michelle's ducking under caused the door to reverse direction, leaving them in plain view of passersby.

Jake moved toward the driver's side, Michelle to the passenger's.

"Agent Jake McCoy of the INS," he called. "Get out of the vehicle slowly, Mr. Evans."

The man inside the car opened the door, then cautiously swung his legs out, his eyes watchful, his hands in the air. "What the hell is going on here?"

Jake took no chances. He thrust his forearm against Gerald's collarbone and shoved him against the side of the car. His gaze locked with the other man's.

Gerald barely blinked as he held his hands higher. "I don't know who you are or what you want, but you should know that my wife heard me pull in and is probably this minute on her way out to greet me."

"Your wife is in Lansing."

Gerald Evans's unhesitant smile made Jake grimace. He was obviously a man used to talking himself out of tight spots, no matter the physical disadvantage. "Yes, I guess she is. So why don't you just let me go so we can talk to each other man to man."

It immediately struck Jake that there was no way he and Gerald could have been any more different. Where he was tall and dark, Gerald Evans was blond and of average height. Where he had an economy with words, Gerald was obviously a master of them, instantly measuring what needed to be said and fitting the words to the situation.

Jake had a hard time seeing this man and Michelle together. But he all too easily understood how Evans had talked her into letting him spend time alone with Lili.

"Where's Lili?" Michelle said as she rounded the vehicle, looking in first one window, then the next.

Gerald went rock still. Jake pressed him harder into the cold metal. "Jesus. You're the last person I expected to see here, Michelle."

"I bet she is." Jake ground the words out, itching to rearrange a few of the guy's pretty-boy features. "Answer her question."

Evans rolled his eyes toward the ceiling and sighed. "I don't have her."

"Where is she?" Michelle repeated, giving up her futile search of the empty vehicle. "Did you drop her off somewhere on your way home?" Her anxious gaze found Jake's. "We should have waited at the airport."

Gerald looked momentarily confused. "What do you know about the airport? And why do you think..." His voice trailed off, realization apparently dawning. "You're probably talking about the companion ticket." His irritating grin drove Jake's impatience level up a couple of notches. "My *wife* was scheduled to go with me. But her father fell ill, and she went to her parents' instead. You should have checked your facts a little more thoroughly."

Jake stared at the man he held prisoner. "Where is she?"

Gerald's eyes were suddenly stony, challenging. Jake noticed the malice lurking there, and knew that nothing short of torturing the guy within an inch of his life would make him give up the information. "I don't have her," he said again.

Michelle started rifling through Gerald's jacket pockets, then peeked in the car window. She opened the door and slid the keys from the ignition.

"Don't mind if we have a little look around your place, do you?" Jake asked, thrusting his arm against Gerald's windpipe.

Gerald gasped. Jake removed his hold, and Gerald bent over double, coughing. Across the garage, Michelle's hands shook violently as she found the right key and unlocked the door.

"Why don't you lead our tour?" Jake suggested, hauling Gerald up by the back of his jacket and thrusting him in the direction Michelle had gone.

Ten minutes later, after a thorough search through the large, four-bedroom house, the three ended up in the kitchen near the garage door entrance. There had been no sign that a child of any age had ever been there. Of the three extra bedrooms, two were empty, one a swanky home office. There were no telltale stains on the pale Berber area rug in the living room. Nothing fit for a child was in the kitchen. No milk or juice in the refrigerator or cereal or canned spaghetti in the pantry.

Michelle looked an inch away from hurtling over the edge of an emotional peak. And Gerald looked far too smug for Jake's liking.

"Awfully big house for one man, wouldn't you say?" Jake said.

"My *wife* and I think it's perfect. Children would only muck it up. In fact, we decided before we even married that we didn't want children."

Jake narrowed his eyes. Then why go through all the trouble to snatch Lili away from her mother? And why stand here as though he couldn't care less where Lili was?

"You know, I forgot to ask for a search warrant," Gerald said, smoothing his jacket.

Jake clenched his jaw so tightly, he was afraid it would shatter. "I'd advise you to shut up right about now."

"Why?" Gerald crossed his arms and leaned easily against the counter. "I legally took Lili from France so I could bring her home, here, to the States. I think even a man such as yourself can understand my desire to have my only child brought up properly, in a safe, nurturing environment."

Michelle overtly eyed an assortment of knives protruding from a wooden block on the counter. Jake pulled her to stand slightly behind him, well away from the deadly instruments.

"Legal by whose standards, Mr. Evans?" Jake asked. "Yours?"

"By our government's standards, Agent McCoy. You should know that better than any one of us here. In fact, why is *she* still in the country? Wasn't her visa due to expire yesterday? Shouldn't she be on a plane bound for France even as we speak?"

The knives started looking awfully good to Jake, as well. "What would you know about Michelle's visa status?"

Gerald shrugged. "Let's just say I've been contacted by someone else from the INS...." His words trailed off, his meaning all too clear.

Jake stared at the man responsible for so much heartbreak. He thought about making one last shot at getting the information they needed out of him. But Gerald's smug grin told him it wouldn't get him anywhere.

"You haven't heard the last from me, Mr. Evans." He grasped Michelle's arm and guided her through the front door.

MICHELLE SAT shivering uncontrollably in the passenger's seat, despite the warmth of the night, despite the jacket Jake had draped over her shoulders.

Gerald's coldness was something she had never expected. No, she hadn't thought he'd just hand Lili over to her, not after having gone through so much to take her. But the malevolence in his eyes had chilled her to the bone. For several long, torturous moments, she'd feared for her daughter's life. The shock of that possibility had never dawned on her, and her oversight made it doubly worse. Could Gerald have harmed Lili? For some sick, demented reason had he decided that he didn't want a child with his blood running through her veins in the world?

Jake's warm fingers threaded through the hair over her left ear, making her realize she was rocking slightly back and forth, clutching Lili's elephant as though clutching her daughter.

"We'll find her, Michelle. This, I promise you."

She gazed at him, wanting to believe him. But she couldn't. Not only couldn't they find Lili—even if they did,

Gerald knew perfectly well that there was nothing they could do to gain immediate custody of her.

A big, hot tear rolled down her cheek, and she violently wiped it away. After speaking to the man who had fathered her child, she knew it was even more important to get Lili away from him. She'd never known him to be so cold, so manipulative.

She didn't realize the car had stopped until she felt Jake's warm breath on her cheek. He'd turned off the four-lane road they'd been on onto a narrow, residential street shadowed by trees, and he'd flipped on the hazard lights.

"Hey?" he murmured, pressing his lips against her cheek, then rubbing his thumb against the dampness there. "Everything's going to be all right. Do you hear me?"

She nodded and bit on her bottom lip.

"No, I don't think you do hear me, Michelle." He hooked his finger under her chin and forced her to face him. She looked everywhere but into his eyes.

Then his mouth brushed hers, once, twice, inviting her to respond. She tightly closed her eyes, a sob gathering in her throat. Jake thrust his fingers through her hair. "Look at me, baby."

She didn't dare.

"Please," he whispered, running his tongue over her bottom lip then nipping at it. "Please look at me, Michelle."

Her eyelids fluttered opened. She felt as if she were looking at him from the bottom of a shallow stream, his features blurry, but there was no mistaking the fiery intensity in his eyes.

Slowly, her vision began to focus. On Jake. On his concern for her. On his closeness. Oh, how she was coming to need this man.

She slid her arms around his neck, looking at him, drinking him in. She pressed her mouth softly against his. She pulled back and looked into his face. How dear he was becoming to her, how vital. At that moment, it was difficult to believe she had survived nearly six whole weeks here without him. Impossible to imagine that she had existed without him for the past twenty-eight years. Worse yet, she couldn't see tomorrow without seeing visions of him coloring the days.

She lifted her hand to his hair, rubbing strands between her fingers, then kissed him again. His quiet groan fed the growing fire within her.

This time when she kissed him, she did so with more urgency. He responded in kind. Then she launched an all-out assault on his mouth, channeling all her churning emotion into the action, pulling at his lips, biting his tongue, unleashing all that swirled within her. He pulled her into his lap, and she shamelessly ground against his erection. She moved her head from left to right, plunging, sucking, gasping for air. And he returned her passion, kiss for kiss, restless caress for caress.

She ripped and pulled at the sweatshirt he wore, and gasped when he slid his fingers under the hem of hers, finding her breasts and plucking at her nipples through the fabric of her bra. Then her bra was loose, and his hot palms covered her. She fumbled for the tie to his drawstring pants and thrust both hands inside his briefs, seeking for and finding his silken erection, sliding her fingers up and down the rock-hard shaft, swallowing his groan. Jake tore at her panties under her short black skirt and shifted so she could straddle him, his mouth never abandoning hers.

Michelle was completely ignorant of the traffic that screamed by on the busy road a mere block away. Didn't want to remember that they were on a residential street, and despite the late hour, passersby could see them. All she knew was an intense desire to have this man inside her *now*.

Jake hauled his mouth from hers, his harsh breathing filling her ear as he rested his forehead against hers. "I...I don't have anything on me."

She kissed the tip of his handsome nose. "We don't need anything," she whispered.

Freeing him from his pants, she thrust her hips forward until her swollen flesh pressed lengthwise along the side of his erection. She shuddered, longing for him to fill her completely but knowing they could give each other pleasure this way. Tilting her hips, she drew her wet heat down the length of him, then back again. Jake groaned against her mouth as she did it again, then again.

The friction of their bodies moving against each other without penetration sent fire racing through Michelle's muscles, chasing the last of the emotional chill away and making her arch her back. Jake immediately took advantage and thrust her shirt over her breasts, then fastened his mouth over one of her jutting nipples. She gripped his shoulders tightly, concentrating on the exquisitely thought-robbing sensation of his velvety shaft resting against her most feminine parts. She slowly, torturously shifted forward, then back.

Jake clutched her hips. "I need to be inside you. Now," he whispered through clenched teeth.

Michelle covered his hands with hers, gasping when he brought the tip of his erection to rest against her opening, his gaze holding hers captive.

She was helpless to stop him. If he was determined to reach penetration.... She moaned, overwhelmed with the need to feel him inside her.

But he didn't enter her. Instead, Jake thrust upward, through her swollen folds, holding her still, holding her hostage as his hips bucked again and again.

Michelle cried out as her body shuddered, the world exploding on the back of her eyelids, even as Jake tensed under her. The feel of the hot evidence of his passion covering her belly sent another round of shock waves rumbling through her. Restlessly, she reached down and raised his hands to her stomach, guiding him to rub the dampness over her skin, her breasts. Reveling in the feel of his passion covering her, the rough skin of his palms rasping against her aching nipples.

She collapsed bonelessly against him, the sound of their ragged breathing filling the car.

Michelle had never felt so dependent on a man before. She knew what it was to love a man completely, with her entire heart, body and soul. Never had someone been so attuned to her needs, her wants. Respecting her even as he demanded from her. So willingly making her pain his. His pleasure hers. His strength hers. And it was from that strength that she would find what she needed to continue her search for Lili.

She slanted her mouth against his, kissing him deeply, passionately. And in his response she sensed he loved her, too.

11

JAKE EMERGED from the bathroom fresh from a shower, fully dressed, his mind swirling with ideas. He opened the curtains, letting in the morning sun. Michelle mumbled something in French then rolled over, pulling a pillow over her tousled head. He grinned, repressing the urge to tug the sheet down over her naked skin, coax her to use her native tongue to drive him wild, then make up for the time they had lost last night after they'd returned to the hotel.

He'd intended his kiss in the car to help clear Michelle's emotion-clouded mind. He couldn't have known it would prove a prelude to much, much more. And the erotic few minutes had also helped clear his mind. Gone was the intense desire to see Gerald Evans take the place of his car hood ornament. In its place was crystal-clear determination, his mind a frighteningly efficient machine as he clicked through every snippet of his and Michelle's conversations over the past few days, and the precious little he'd gained from her file when it had been open on Brad's desk. He ignored the niggling in the back of his brain that reminded him there was still much he didn't know in that file. That didn't apply to the here and now. What did was finding Lili before Edgar found them.

He managed to squeeze in an hour of sleep at some point, but between holding Michelle as she cried in her sleep and murmured words in French he didn't understand, and his need to do something, he'd been awake most of the night.

Suddenly, Michelle bolted upright in bed, the sheet falling from her delectable breasts, her hair sexily tousled around her head. Jake was instantly struck with the desire to kiss her, to finish what they'd begun in the car the night before. He hadn't been able to after returning to the hotel because he'd come out of the shower last night to find her sleeping fitfully.

A knock sounded at the door. Michelle looked at him, the concern on her face evident as she clutched the sheet to her chest. Jake peered through the peephole, then opened the door.

"Thanks for coming so quickly."

The hotel employee glanced from Jake to Michelle, then set up an elaborate, state-of-the-art laptop computer on the table near the phone. Within moments, it was booted up, connected to the phone line and ready to go.

Jake walked him to the door and tipped him generously before closing and bolting the door.

"What's...what's this?" Michelle asked, endearingly confused.

"A laptop computer."

"You can get one of these from the hotel?"

He grinned. "Yes, they allow you to borrow them."

Another knock. This time Michelle bolted into the bathroom. Jake stared after her firm little bottom as she zoomed by, then adjusted himself in his sweatpants. For God's sake, what the woman did to him without even trying. He opened the door again, and this time a cart crammed full of breakfast dishes was rolled in. By the time Michelle came out of the bathroom, freshly showered and wrapped in that silly, sexy robe, Jake was sitting at the computer munching on a piece of toast. She stopped in front of the cart. "This is breakfast?"

"Uh-huh. I didn't know what you liked, so I ordered everything."

She fingered the top of an open champagne bottle in an ice bucket.

He looked away. "Compliments of the hotel."

"Ah."

"I asked them for that latte thing you like."

A sound of deep satisfaction emerged from her throat. She sat cross-legged on the bed behind his chair and picked up the soup-bowl-size cup, doing the human equivalent of purring as she took her first sip.

"What are you going to do?" she asked, lapping cream from her upper lip.

Jake tore his gaze from the painfully erotic flick of her tongue and turned to the computer. He accessed his ISP account with a D.C. carrier then gained access to a special reverse directory only certain government investigators could employ to seek out addresses. Whatever Edgar was up to, it thankfully hadn't affected his ability to access the data. "What's your number in Paris?"

"My number?"

God, but he wanted to touch her. Massage the worried lines from between her expressive brown eyes. Whisper things into her ear that would make her forget the gravity of their search. But while making love to her would work for a little while, afterward they would crash down to earth to find themselves right where they were when they started. Actually, in a worse situation, because an invisible clock was ticking. By now Edgar had likely gotten the documentation needed to pull both him and Michelle in. It was only a matter of time before he found them and pulled the rug from under their feet.

He opened his mouth, prepared to ask Michelle exactly what was hidden in the shadows of her past that made her rate a spot so high on the INS hit list. Then fear forced his question down. It didn't matter, anyway. The information wouldn't change their situation. It would only cloud his judgment, take his mind from the matter at hand.

"You said that Lili knew her home phone number, right? That it was just recently she was taught of the dangers of abduction. It's more than likely she'd been trying to call you, but—"

"But because she doesn't know the correct area code, or understand overseas calling procedures—"

"She probably got a local number instead," Jake confirmed.

Michelle sat straighter, her eyes alight with new hope. God, how he wanted to kiss her.

She clearly repeated her phone number for him. He entered it into the search engine. A moment later, a message popped up informing him there was no such number in that area code. Jake sat back and rubbed his fingers against his eyelids.

"Wait!" Michelle said before he exited the system, her mouth filled with a strawberry. "She always transposed the last two numbers! Try it."

He did. Within moments, a name and number popped up. Jake wrote them down. Michelle wiped her sticky hands on a napkin then picked up the phone and began dialing. Jake reached over and depressed the disconnect button.

"What? We need to call the number, yes? See if Lili has been trying to contact me?"

He tapped the face of his watch. "I don't think you're going to find Ms. Hagan very cooperative right now. It's only eight on a Wednesday morning."

"Oh." Lethargically, Michelle replaced the receiver.

"Anyway, I think it better if we visit in person a little later this morning. It's too easy for someone to give you the brush-off over the phone. Face-to-face, they tend to make a little more effort to help you."

He turned to the computer and checked the listing of area codes in the tri-state area. Noting Lansing's, where Gerald's wife was supposedly staying with her parents, and the surrounding ones, he jotted them down and did a search using the phone number with each of the area codes. Only one came through as a legitimate number. It belonged to an antique shop in Napolean, Ohio. Michelle reached for the phone again.

"It's a business, no? Which means they may be open?"

Jake grinned. "Yes."

She started to dial, hesitated, then handed the phone to him. "I don't think I can handle it."

He accepted the receiver, then folded his fingers over hers. He met her eyes meaningfully, then tugged her until she was sitting on his lap.

He'd done it to allow her to listen in on the conversation. But the instant welcome a certain body part gave to the close proximity of Michelle's hot bottom was something he hadn't anticipated.

Her smile was downright naughty as she dialed the last number. "There."

Jake quickly put the receiver to his ear.

An elderly male answered the phone. Jake spent five minutes on the phone with him, going over all the possibilities. Had a little girl called asking for her *maman* in French? No. Were there other employees who answered the phone? No. Sometimes it helped to keep the person on the line, so Jake asked how the antiques business was going and got an earful on the topic. But when he returned to the subject of Lili, he was told the only strange call the old man had gotten recently was from some fast-talking salesman trying to sell him foreign lottery tickets. Jake advised him to pass on the deal, then hung up the receiver.

Michelle crossed the name off the short list, then got up

and went to sit on the bed. Idly she picked at the food on the cart. "No Lili."

Jake plucked a strawberry from a bowl and held it out to her. She glanced at him from under her thick lashes, her heart so clearly in her eyes it caused his own to constrict. He was about to pull the fruit back when she moved her lips around it, then bit into it with her straight little teeth. He swallowed before she did, watching as juice ran down the side of her mouth and over her chin. She chewed slowly, watching him. He realized he was making the same chewing motion and groaned. God, it was inhuman, the need he felt for this woman.

Glancing at the clock and seeing that they didn't have anything more to do for a couple hours, he grabbed the bowl of strawberries and the bottle of champagne and practically dove on top of her on the bed.

NOTHING. Not a single one of the numbers panned out. Either Lili hadn't been given access to a phone, or she hadn't tried to call.

Michelle sat cradling her coffee cup in concentration. The ticking of a clock in her ears grew louder with each passing minute and with each dead end she and Jake reached. She'd experienced so many highs and lows over the past three days, she didn't quite know where she was. She only knew where she would be soon. In Paris. Without her daughter.

She glanced at Jake, who sat opposite her, his gaze intense on her. She shivered. His want of her physically was lurking in his warm gray eyes, but so was something else. More than curiosity, almost suspicion.

She looked around the small diner near the Ohio Michigan border. Most of the lunch customers had left, leaving her and Jake nearly alone in the corner booth.

"So what do we do now?" she whispered, afraid of his answer.

He didn't answer. It appeared he hadn't heard her.

She put her cup down and pushed her hardly eaten lasagna away.

"There's one other area we have yet to check," he said quietly.

She searched his face, hardly daring to hope that there was another option.

"Gerald's parents' place."

Despite her best efforts, hope ran away with her. "Of course!" Her mind raced. "We have to go through there to get back to..." She allowed her words to trail off, not able to say "back to D.C." "It's only a couple of hours away, yes? That means we can be there before five. A good time to check into strange callers, yes?"

The smile he gave her was decidedly less bright than ones he'd honored her with before. "Yes."

"Then let's go!"

She pulled him up, barely giving him time to put money down for the bill before she tugged him to the car.

The scenery went by more quickly this time. Michelle made herself look at it: the deep greens, the kiss of autumn on some trees. Ignoring the hum of the air conditioner, she pushed the automatic window opener then took a deep breath of the late summer air. Jake shut off the air and rolled down his window, his short hair tousling in the wind. She smiled at him with her entire being.

The landscape was so unlike where she'd grown up in southern France. The land was flat and seemed to stretch out to forever. She noticed a cow farm, and her smile widened. How little Lili would have loved to see the cows. She could envision her daughter making their mooing sound and pointing at the animals several times to make sure Michelle had seen them.

Before too long, they rolled into the small town of Canton, where their search had begun only the day before, but it seemed so very long ago. Jake got out of the car and used a pay phone to call information, then minutes later pulled into a copy center that offered Internet access. Before she knew it, he had the addresses he needed. One number was unlisted. But the number with the last two digits transposed wasn't that far from where they were.

Michelle tried to relax as they drove the short way. She caught herself twisting her wedding band around her finger, then looked at Jake's hand. He still wore his band, as well. The realization made her feel better. Not so alone, despite the unexplained somber expression he wore.

Jake pulled to a stop, staring out the window at a two-apartment dwelling. He referred to the slip of paper he held, then looked at her. "Are you ready?"

For a long moment, she was unable to move. This was it. If the owner hadn't received any unusual calls in the past eight weeks...

She nodded, then reached for the door knocker, fervently praying in her native French. Please let them know something. Please....

A woman answered the door, a cigarette hanging from her fleshy lips, her hair in steel-colored curlers, her flowered housecoat stained and faded. "Whaddaya want?"

Jake held out his business card and introduced himself then explained the situation. Michelle held her breath, afraid to move, afraid to speak for fear that it would result in bad news or the slamming of the door in their faces.

"French?" the woman repeated. "What do I know from French?"

Michelle looked beyond her to where a teenage girl lay across an old sofa, the telephone receiver attached to her ear.

"No, we haven't gotten any unusual calls."

"Are you sure?" Michelle asked. "Maybe your daughter—"

"That's my niece. And I'm sure. Now I've got something cooking on the stove."

She began to turn away. Jake said, "Do you mind if we speak to your niece?"

The woman's expression turned decidedly suspicious. "Yes, I do mind. Now get out of here before I call the police."

"Good Lord, Aunt Bert, can you keep it down to a low roar? I'm on the phone!" The girl got up from the sofa and disappeared from sight.

The woman named Bert slammed the door firmly in their faces.

Michelle stood paralyzed. That was it. No new leads on Lili and her possible whereabouts.

Jake gripped her arms. "Are you all right?"

Michelle realized she had nearly fallen over before he'd steadied her. She slowly nodded, but when the action caused dizziness, shook it instead. "I think I'm going to be sick."

He led her to the side of the house where a stand of bushes hid her from sight as she retched up what little she'd eaten at lunch.

"Aunt Bert's gonna have a heart attack if she finds out."

Michelle ran the back of her hand across her mouth and looked up to find the teenage girl leaning on a window ledge above her. She explained to whomever she was talking to on the phone that some woman had just hurled all over her aunt's front yard. "You drunk or something?" she asked Michelle.

Jake handed Michelle his handkerchief. "No, she's not drunk." He eyed the girl. "That phone have a double line?"

The girl frowned. "Double line? No. But it has call waiting, if that's what you mean."

His smile returned, and Michelle felt her heart give a little jump in her chest.

"You stay here a lot?"

"I live here."

"With your aunt?"

"Yeah, ever since Mom went into detox. Again." She moved the receiver to her mouth. "Hold on a sec, Melinda, can't you hear I'm talking to someone?"

Aunt Bert's loud voice sounded through the window. Michelle jumped, then realized she wasn't anywhere near. She was calling her niece for dinner.

Jake slid his hand in his pocket and took out a small pile of dollars in different denominations he pretended an interest in sorting. "What's your name?"

"Stacy," the girl said slowly. "Why?"

"You answer the phone a lot, Stacy?"

The girl's focus was strictly on the money. "All the time."

"Probably because you don't get much by way of allowance so you can go out and...do things that girls your age do."

"So?"

Jake slid a twenty from the small stack. "You get any unusual calls lately?"

"Maybe."

Michelle's throat tightened.

"From whom?" Jake held out the money.

"Who? From these stupid dweebs from school, that's who." The girl tried to take the money, but Jake pulled his hand back.

"I mean from someone you don't know, say in the past eight weeks or so, from a little girl."

Stacy frowned again. "Let me call you back, Melinda."

She hung up the receiver then sat with her hands resting against the body of the phone possessively. "You know, it's really weird that you ask that. Do you know her? Because like it really freaked me out, you know? I mean the first time she called, I thought it was one of my friends playing a practical joke, but then she called again, and I got this weird feeling that something was wrong with her, you know? Because she was crying and everything. Then a couple weeks ago, the calls, like, stopped—"

A sob burst from Michelle's throat, and she put her hands over her mouth to quell it.

"She all right, man?"

Jake's grin was one-hundred-percent pure satisfaction. "Yes, she's all right. Thanks, Stacy. Thank you very much." He handed her the twenty, then carefully led Michelle to the car.

JAKE GLANCED to where Michelle had her fist over her mouth to stop sobbing. He suppressed his desire to celebrate. Knowing Gerald's parents had had the girl was a long way from his and Michelle's chances of recovering her. Besides, Stacy had said the calls had stopped a couple of weeks back. It could have been because her grandparents had caught on to what Lili was doing. Or because she'd assimilated and no longer felt the need to call her mother. Or, worse, had given up any hope of her mother finding her. Or, worst of all, she could have moved somewhere else.

Jake turned the corner onto the Evanses' street and immediately jammed on the brakes. He didn't have to explain to Michelle. She was also staring at the dark blue sedan parked two blocks up. *Edgar.*

"Damn," he muttered.

He put the car in reverse and he backed up until the car was completely blocked from sight.

"What's he doing here?" Michelle whispered.

He could have responded in any number of ways. Told her that since they'd lost him in Toledo, Edgar's best chance of finding them was by camping out here because it was likely Gerald had told Edgar of Lili's whereabouts. He could have said he didn't know. He could have told her not to worry.

But he did none of them. Instead, he put the car in park and started to get out.

"Listen to me carefully, Michelle. I want you to drive two blocks up then turn left. Park between two cars if you can, preferably under some trees. Wait there for me."

She reached out and grabbed his arm desperately. "Do you think Lili's there?"

"That's what I'm going to find out."

He gently pried her fingers from his arm, but before he closed the door, he curved his hand over the side of her face. She instantly closed her eyes and leaned into his touch, making him want to groan.

There were so many conflicting emotions crowding his chest, he didn't know what to do. He withdrew his hand then closed the door, motioning for her to go. She did so, slowing after she cleared the cross street, likely watching him in the rearview mirror. He turned the corner and shoved his hands deep into the pockets of his sweats.

The feel of the unfamiliar material reminded him that he should be somewhere in the backwoods of the Blue Ridge Mountains right now, devising ways to make David pay for dragging him out there. Instead, he was falling head over heels in love with a woman who was turning his life upside down. Searching for her daughter with only this one hope of finding her. And it was eating his gut not knowing what secret lurked in Michelle's past, a secret serious enough to have Edgar tailing her for two straight days.

He didn't bother pretending he didn't see his fellow agent. He strode to the side of the car and rapped on the closed window.

Edgar jumped, having been slumped over catching a nap. Then he scrambled to get out of the car. "For God's sake, McCoy, you could have given me a freakin' heart attack."

"Yeah, well, consider it down payment on the large debt I owe you."

Edgar frowned at him. "Did you just crack a joke, McCoy?"

Jake ignored him and looked at the house across the street. "How long have you known the little girl's been here?"

"Since last night." Edgar straightened his suit coat. "Only she's not there anymore. Grandparents took off with her yesterday morning, right after you and the Frenchwoman left."

"It's Michelle." Jake stared at him. "Any idea where they went?"

He shrugged. "Could be just about anywhere, considering the resources these guys have. East coast, west coast. Seeing as the girl has a legal American passport, they might even have left the country. And seeing as the old man is retired..."

Jake ran his hand over his face, suppressing the desire to hit Edgar. But coldcocking Edgar wouldn't get him anywhere, because his fellow agent was completely right. There was no telling where they'd gone, or when, if ever, they'd be back.

Not that it mattered. If the agent next to him had a say, Michelle would be heading to France soon anyway.

"So where's the French...Ms. Lambert?" Edgar asked, scanning the street.

Jake shrugged. "Could be anywhere. East coast. West."

Edgar squinted at him in the setting sun. "That would be funny except I know you never joke, and this is no laughing matter."

"Yeah."

"You know your ass is in trouble, don't you? I mean, she's told you why we refused her extension request?"

Jake narrowed his gaze on the other man, his chest tightening in apprehension.

He'd wanted to ask Michelle directly about what marred her record. Wanted her to be the one to tell him, help him understand. But if the past day was any indication of how long it would take him to get around to it, he'd never find out.

"Yeah, I know," he lied.

Edgar's burst of laughter surprised him. "Sure you do, old boy. Sure you do."

Jake was caught between needing to go and needing to stay. He glanced up the street. His car, of course, was nowhere in sight. Michelle would be sitting where he'd instructed her to, scared spitless, waiting for him to return.

"So you going to arrest me?" he asked.

"Naw, you know I wouldn't do that. Not without the woman here, anyway."

Jake figured as much. He nodded and began walking away.

"Hey, McCoy, during time outs, you know, from all that hot and heavy sex you're probably having with her, why don't you try asking her about Blue Earth and a bunch of highly classified naval documents that came up missing in San Francisco about ten years ago?"

Jake forced himself to keep moving. To act as if what Edgar said didn't hit him like a blow to the gut. To pretend it didn't matter that what hid in Michelle's past was probably worse than anything he'd imagined.

The problem was, it did matter to him, deeply.

12

It was the following morning when Jake finally pulled into the driveway of the old McCoy place. His eyelids felt leaden, his body anesthetized as he switched the ignition off and sat staring at the transformed house. As they said they would, Mitch and Liz had erected an ornate iron archway at the end of the driveway, supported by foundations of new red brick. Spelled out at the top was Red Shoe Ranch.

He looked to where Michelle slept fitfully next to him, her cheeks paler than ever, her curled-up position both defensive and defenseless. She'd said Lili's name several times during the night and startled herself awake, only to find that nothing had changed; they were still heading to D.C.

Only Jake hadn't taken her to D.C. He'd brought her here.

He looked at the house. He really didn't know why he'd driven here or what he hoped to accomplish by bringing Michelle. If he had a brain in his head, he'd take her to the airport and put her on the first airplane out. Then again, if he had a brain in his head, he would have found out why the INS wanted her out of the country so badly.

If his three-year stretch in the Marines so long ago had taught him anything, it was the importance of protecting one's borders. Not just from the enemies without, but also from the enemies within. Posted for fifteen long months in a war-torn Third World country, one experience stood out starkly from the others: the day he'd watched an old lady try to cross the border. She needed the help of a cane to walk, each of her wrinkles telling a different story of hardship and pain, and appeared to pose a danger to no one. Then a search found that she carried bricks of plastic explosives strapped to her body, hidden by oversize housecoats and a shawl—explosives that would have killed people of her own country had they gotten through, all because of a difference in theologies.

The experience had twisted Jake's gut. It had also made that much easier his decision about which law enforcement branch to work in when he got home.

Knowing he had not only failed in his job, but had wittingly allowed someone who possibly posed a threat to his country, his home—no matter how he felt about her—to remain there for a prolonged length of time, sat like acid in his stomach.

A voice in the back of his mind told him that he was overreacting, that the hurting woman next to him who was murmuring her daughter's name in her sleep couldn't possibly pose a threat to anybody, much less the big, bad United States of America. But he refused to lie to himself anymore, refused to continue to play the fool as he had so willingly the past few days.

"Then what the hell are you doing here, McCoy?" he muttered, realizing that he'd brought that same threat home, straight to his family's doorstep. He should have taken her to his apartment in Woodley Park—where Edgar probably would have knocked on the door quicker than they could have closed it.

Michelle stirred at the sound of his voice at the same time that Mitch's old dog, Goliath, spotted the car and issued a short but loud series of barks.

"Where...where are we?" Michelle asked, her accent thick, her heavy-lidded eyes sultry. Jake tried to ignore how sexy she looked. That was what had gotten him into trouble in the first place.

Yeah, like he had put up a fight. Not only had he given in, he'd given in over and over and over again. He didn't think there was a time in his life when he'd made love to a woman so often in such a short span of time and so...thoroughly. Not that it mattered. He was filled with the urge to press her back against the seat and have at her all over again. It was time he started thinking with his brain rather than other parts of his anatomy.

"The house I grew up in," he said. "Come on, get your stuff. I'll take you inside so you can get some sleep."

He felt her gaze on him, much as he'd periodically felt it on him during the long drive home. He sensed that she knew something was wrong, but she hadn't asked him what—which was just as well, because he likely wouldn't have told her. He needed time to get his thoughts together, time to get used to the idea that the woman he thought he knew so well was in fact very different. He reached for the door handle, inexplicably relieved when she did the same on the other side.

Goliath began to jump, but one look from Jake sent his mammoth paws to the ground. He really didn't know why everyone else had a discipline problem with the pooch. Goliath always behaved well around Jake.

Spotting Michelle, the slobber puss sprang for her, stamping paw prints over the front of her shirt, his furry butt waggling back and forth wildly along with his bushy tail.

"*Merde*," Michelle said, though the smile on her face revealed her true feelings. Jake ordered the dog down, and Goliath immediately obeyed, sitting at Michelle's feet and whining.

"Come on, let's go inside." Jake turned toward the door then stopped. It was just after dawn, and he'd hoped they could sneak in without notice. No such luck. The front steps were jammed full of McCoy males and two McCoy females.

Jake grimaced and rubbed his forehead as he led the way toward the silent group. He really wasn't up for this. There would be questions. There would be answers. Then there would be more questions. And if he wasn't careful, his sisters-in-law Melanie and Liz would be planning a wedding for him and Michelle in no time.

He slowly moved his hand from his forehead, realizing he already was married. Worse, he was still wearing the wedding ring. Damn. The last thing he wanted was for these guys to know what was going on straight from the start. There were things he needed to do, calls that needed to be made.

He and Michelle finally stopped near the foot of the stairs. Jake cleared his throat as seven pairs of eyes looked back and forth between them. "This is, um, Michelle," he said. "My wife."

Holy mother of God, Jesus and Joseph! Had he just said what he thought he had? Judging by the wide eyes, dropped jaws and a couple of groans he got, yes, he very much indeed had said it. Even Michelle stared at him in openmouthed shock.

"Hi...good morning," Michelle said from next to him, pushing her purse strap on her shoulder, looking about ready to bolt.

Not that he could blame her. If he'd been given a second, he would have been leading the way.

"Oh, she is French!" Liz was the first to regain her composure as she jostled her way through the crowd to approach Michelle. "Hi, I'm Liz. And the other lone female over there is Melanie. It's a—" her gaze strayed to Jake, a knowing twinkle in her eyes "—pleasure to meet you, Michelle. Welcome to the family."

Behind her, Sean cleared his throat. Jake berated himself again for having brought Michelle home, but for entirely different reasons than before. He hadn't even thought of how his family might interpret his actions. Okay, so he had never brought a woman home before, but this was different. Michelle wasn't a woman. He cringed. Of course she was a woman, but not just any woman. And now that he had introduced her as his wife...

Ah, hell, who was he trying to kid? It was one thing being on the road with her, just the two of them. Quite another to be here, being judged by the only people who had ever really mattered in his life. Truth was, he didn't quite know what he was feeling. A part of him wanted to step in front of Michelle, protect her from curious McCoy eyes. Another wanted to take his words back, explain exactly what he meant by *wife*. But when it came down to it, he was completely incapable of doing either.

Liz looked at him meaningfully, then took Michelle by the arm. "Come on. Let me introduce you to the rest of the McCoy clan. Oh, and don't let all that testosterone scare you. They may be all rough and tough when it comes to the law, but they're all just a bunch of softies when it comes to the fairer sex."

"Softies?" Connor echoed, grimacing.

Liz smiled at him, then leaned closer to Michelle. "Okay, most of them are. Connor and David here still like to think themselves immune, but Mel and I are working on it."

Jake didn't miss how easy it was for her to exclude him from that dwindling group of bachelor McCoys. He opened his mouth to correct her, to tell her that he was still very much a bachelor, then he caught Pops staring at the ring on his finger. Judging by the heat of his face, Jake suspected he turned fifty kinds of red. His father lifted his gaze. The grin Sean gave him nearly knocked him over.

Liz continued with her introductions. "This here is the family patriarch, Sean. But none of us call him that. He's Pops to us." She motioned to where Connor stood at the top of the stairs, his arms crossed over his denim-clad chest. "The old hardie up there is Connor, the oldest. Next to him, that cutie is Mitch, my guy." Her smile nearly spread across the whole of her face. "Where was I? Oh, yes. See the one next to Mel? That's her husband, Marc." She leaned closer to Michelle to add in a lower voice, "They've been arguing, so don't pay them any mind—something about Marc being assigned to protect one of the presidential candidates. He's Secret Service. Oh, and the blond one over there with the Brad Pitt good looks? That's David, the baby of the family." David snorted even as he grinned his hello. "Never mind him. He's not too happy right now, either, because Jake was supposed to go hiking with him this week." Liz turned her smile on Michelle. "Looks like Jake had more interesting things on his agenda, though."

Jake grimaced. If Liz only knew the half of it.

Aggravated, he waved toward the house. "Why don't you take Michelle inside and show her to my old room. I..." What? Need to get as far from here as humanly possible? "Um, I need to go get something out of the car."

Michelle looked at him as Liz led her through the throng of bone and muscle on the stairs, Mel instantly taking her other arm when they reached the top. Jake didn't miss the shadow of grief in Michelle's brown eyes when she saw Mel's girth, the baby she carried grown larger every time he saw her. He also didn't miss his wash of guilt at having abandoned her to the well-wishing but overwhelming attentions of his sisters-in-law.

He cleared his throat then turned toward the car. As soon as he'd moved a couple of feet, he pulled and twisted at his wedding band, covertly trying to work it from his finger. The sucker wouldn't budge. Goliath caught up with him, his tongue lolling from the side of his mouth as Jake frowned at him.

"Quite a looker, your Michelle," Pops said, coming up on the other side of Goliath.

"A little on the short side, isn't she?" Connor said, coming up on Jake's other side.

David popped up next to him. "They've always said dynamite comes in small packages."

"Yeah, and if it's one thing Pops always tried to drill into you, it's to stay away from explosives. You'd best remember that," Connor said.

Jake curled his fingers into fists. He wanted to tell them all to leave him alone so he could sort everything out, figure out where to go from here. But he knew better. The moment he asked them to leave, they'd only stay longer. "Anyway, it's nothing like that," he said. *Liar*. It was exactly like that. Michelle's combustible response to him was exactly the reason he was in this mess.

Jake looked at Mitch as they neared the car. He couldn't quite make out what his younger brother was thinking. It wasn't too long ago that Jake had called Mitch's relationship with Liz into question. While Mitch had never been the vengeful type, it didn't make sense that he wouldn't say something, anything, now.

They reached the car. Jake made a show of opening the trunk.

"So tell us what it is like, then," Connor said, leaning against the side of the car and crossing his arms.

Jake rifled through his backpack, not really looking for anything but not wanting to look at the only brother who was older than him, either. Connor had always been what his high-school English teacher had called a Nosey Parker. Jake couldn't count the scrapes he and Connor had gotten into over the span of their lifetimes. From something as simple as what to fix for breakfast to what they should do about Marc, who was always getting into some sort of trouble or other when they were younger, anything was capable of setting them off. Ultimately, though, Jake had usually conceded. Not because he thought Connor was right, but because it wasn't worth more than a couple of jabs.

"It's complicated," Jake muttered.

David poked around inside the trunk and spotted the backpack. "Hey, you really were going to come hiking, weren't you? Are those Timberland? Good Lord, Jake, you really went top of the line, didn't you?" David absently tugged the backpack from Jake's grip. His chuckle somehow lightened the atmosphere. "Look at this. All the things a guy needs for survival in the wilderness." He quirked a brow at Jake, holding up a book. "Did you really think I'd make you eat moss?"

Jake snatched the book. "It was a possibility."

"I'm crushed."

"You'll get over it."

Pops cleared his throat. "She seems like a nice enough girl."

Jake stuffed the book into his pack then looked at his father. "She's a woman, Pops, through and through. And yes, she is nice—straightforward, fresh, um, nice." He felt his face go hot again. "When she talks, I know where she's coming from, you know? And she…gets me. Most of the women I date…um, dated, thought something was wrong if I wasn't talking a mile a minute. Not Michelle. We can sit for hours without a word passing between us—"

Connor barked a laugh. "Probably because she doesn't know English well enough to carry on a—"

"Her English is better than yours, Con of the Jungle."

His four brothers and father went silent. Judging by their

open-eyed expressions, Jake pretty much figured he'd shocked the hell out of them.

Sean squeezed his shoulder. "I don't think I've ever heard you say so many words before in one breath."

David laughed. "Yeah, and I wouldn't exactly say wit is one of your stronger suits, but what you just said to Connor... Well, let's just say that since your jaw's still attached, he must not have expected it, either."

The six of them laughed, Jake included.

Marc shrugged. "Hey, whatever trips your trigger, you know? And after getting a look at her...well, I can certainly see where she'd be capable of doing that."

Mitch frowned at Marc. Jake was reminded again that Mitch had yet to say anything about the situation. He'd yet to do anything more than smile when it was expected. Jake didn't know why, but he had the feeling his brother had something to share that wasn't along the lines of, "You did what?"

Sean sighed and looked at the house. "Yeah, well, I think we've busted poor Jake's chops enough, guys. What say we leave him to his business and get in to that, um, breakfast the McCoy women have scared up for us?"

"Scared being the operative word," Connor grumbled, stuffing his hands deep in his jeans pockets. He gave Jake a sidelong look, shrugged, then started toward the house.

David hefted the backpack out of the trunk. "Mind if I look through this stuff?"

Jake waved him off. "Go ahead. Just know I have an inventory of everything in there."

Marc chuckled then put a headlock on their youngest brother as they sauntered away.

Only Pops and Mitch remained. Pops gave Mitch a long glance, but Mitch ignored him and pretended an interest in the old barn that stood hulking in the right front corner of the property.

Pops sighed. "Okay, obviously you two have something to discuss. Just don't be too long, or else Liz'll have both your butts in a sling." He started to step away, then stopped. "You do remember what day it is, Jake?"

Jake stared at his father, searching his memory. Then it hit him. It was the anniversary of their mother's death. He nodded solemnly.

"We thought we'd head over to the site around eleven. That okay with you?"

"Yeah."

Finally, he and Mitch were alone. Jake closed the trunk and looked at his younger brother curiously.

"Come on, let's go see how the horses are doing," Mitch said, draping an arm around his shoulders.

Jake ground his teeth together. Why the dramatics? He had the sinking sensation that he was being led to the slaughter. Then he realized that Mitch must know what he'd found out from Edgar, which shouldn't have surprised him. When he'd called Mitch the day before, he should have known he'd do some checking around on his own. And considering the nature of the information, the FBI would be the perfect place to do that checking.

Jake sighed. Normally, he would wait for Mitch to do the talking. But he couldn't stand the silence a moment longer. "Look, Mitch, I know what you're going to say. And while I appreciate your concern, this is really something I have to work out by myself."

The wide-eyed look was something Jake should be growing accustomed to by now, but the truth was, it wasn't an expression he was used to inspiring. He didn't think it ever would be. "Fair enough," his brother said, finally.

They entered the new barn, the sharp and subtle odors assaulting Jake's nose as fresh straw crunched underfoot. One of the stallions nickered, and Mitch reached into a pail near the door for a cube of sugar to feed him.

"So you know all you have riding on the line here, then, huh?"

Jake nodded, wishing he had his brother's touch with animals. Just like with children, animals tended to be wary of him, afraid. Why, he wasn't sure. Maybe it was because he never fawned over them the way his brother did. Hesitantly, he reached out for a few cubes of sugar, the grainy feel a new one against his skin. He held his hand out to the sleek black stallion whose nameplate read Seti.

"Lower your hand a little and bring it in a little closer," Mitch said quietly.

Jake did so. The horse smelled it first with his cool nose, then lapped the cube up with infinite skill. Jake frowned at the wet mess he left behind. Mitch laughed and handed him a towel. "Never were much for getting dirty, were you, Jake?"

"That's not dirt, that's slime."

Mitch slapped him on the back and led him down the aisle.

"So...how's married life treating you?" Jake asked, hoping to encourage their conversation away from himself and Michelle.

"Liz and I are doing just fine." Mitch shrugged. "She insists the color I painted the office is not the color she requested. Hell, I tell her, what's the difference between magenta and eggplant, anyway? Then there's this discussion about kids. I want them now, she thinks it's too soon. Says I should content myself with being an uncle to Marc and Mel's baby for the time being." His grin was infectious. "She also won't even consider going above two kids."

Jake hiked a brow. "You want more?"

Mitch nodded, looking a little gob-smacked. "Yeah, I do. Funny, isn't it? I never really gave it a great deal of thought until after I finally roped Liz in. Now I want to pop as many out as we can. I don't think there's anything more exciting than the thought of ten or twelve little Lizzes running around the place."

Jake nearly choked.

"Okay, maybe four or five."

"You know, you're just as likely to get another batch of stubborn McCoy males."

"Yeah, I know." He tightened his grip on Jake's shoulder. "That wouldn't be so bad, would it? The place could do with a few more strapping males. Of course, my first choice would be a little girl, one who preferably would wear those cute little pink dresses and shriek if she so much as got her black patent leather shoes dirty."

Jake smiled at the image, only in his mind he superimposed little Lili's face on the girl in question.

He cleared his throat, realizing he didn't have a clue what Lili was like. Was she like her mother? Was she affectionate, playful, able to tell a joke as well as get one? Was she sweet and feminine, leaning toward all things frilly?

"Gotta tell you something, though, Jake," Mitch said as he led them out the other side of the new construction. "I never thought you would beat us all to the fatherhood bit."

"Fatherhood?" Jake nearly croaked.

Mitch smiled at him. "Of course. You realize that you are officially a stepfather now, right? That Elizabeth—"

"Lili," he automatically corrected.

"Okay then, Lili. You know that the moment you married her mother, you essentially took on the role of her father. Well, a father once removed, but from what I saw listed on her real father... Well, let's just say you're her father."

"Father?" Jake felt like an idiot for repeating Mitch so often, but he couldn't think of anything else to say. Yes, while he'd married Michelle to help her stay in the country long enough to find Lili, he'd never stopped to consider what that meant for her daughter...his daughter.

He suddenly felt light-headed.

"What's the matter, Jake? You all right?"

"Yeah." He grinned stupidly. He was all right. More than all right, he felt proud, somehow. Which was even dumber, given their circumstances. But just the thought of a little girl out there needing a father, and him being legally in line for the job... "Wonder if this is the way Marc feels. You're right, of course. Lili is now my daughter, even though I've never met her."

Mitch chuckled quietly. "Difference is, you're going to get to skip all those slimy diapers."

Jake laughed. Then laughed again. Then laughed so damned hard he nearly bent over double.

Good Lord, he was a daddy....

MICHELLE WALKED around Jake's room, then walked around it again. Most might think the room revealed little about the boy who had once inhabited it. She smiled. She thought it revealed everything.

The narrow bed in the middle of the room was covered by a blue broad plaid patterned spread, the curtains at the windows made from the same fabric. The old desk in the corner was completely clean, likely everything tucked away in the drawers, a place for everything and everything in its place. The bookshelves were neat, the books lined up by size rather than by author. She stepped closer. *Tom Sawyer* sat right alongside Clancy. She fingered a small, tarnished statue of a cowboy, strong and silent. She ran her thumb over the somber features then put it down.

She told herself she should feel out of place here, in this

strange room, in this foreign place, but she didn't. Jake was everywhere. In every corner. In every crease in the curtains. Surrounding her. Filling her.

She moved to the window. Jake was coming out of a low building with his brother...Mitch, she recalled. Her heart did an immediate somersault in her chest. Oh, how she loved this man. And the thought that she soon wouldn't be able to see him...

She wouldn't think about that, refused to think about that.

She hugged her arms around herself and listened to the sound of laughter coming from downstairs. His family was just as she imagined. Cohesive. The type that gathered on Sundays, like today, for dinner. Breakfast was a rarity, Liz had told her when she'd brought her upstairs, but what with everything that was happening with Jake... Well, last night found them all gathered at the house waiting for word.

She couldn't imagine growing up in such an environment. While her mother was alive, it had been just her father, mother and her. Then there had been Dad and Jacqueline, then later, three more children. But there was never the closeness so evident in the family downstairs. Everyone in her family had always had their own agendas. Her step siblings had school activities, Jacqueline was busy with her interests, and while Michelle and her father occasionally managed to grab a meal out together, it wasn't the same thing. The ghost of her mother always seemed to be hovering somewhere nearby.

She remembered that Jake, as well, had lost his mother. But rather than rip the family apart, it appeared to have drawn them closer together.

A brief knock sounded at the door. Thinking it was Jake, she told him to enter.

"Hi," Liz said. "I didn't know if you'd still be up. Jake said you two were on the road pretty much all night. But I just wanted to bring you up a plate of food, you know, in case you were hungry." She set a tray on the clean desktop, then turned and smiled. "If you're not tired, you can always come down and join us."

"Thanks. Maybe I will."

Liz held out a small bag. "I'm sure you probably have everything you need, but I gathered some things you might want. There's a toothbrush, toothpaste, nightgown." Her smile was decidedly wicked. "If you're anything like me, you never wore much to bed before. In this place, though, you never know who'll be walking through the door."

Michelle laughed, deciding she liked this Liz McCoy, wife of Mitch. "Thanks."

Liz looked around the room. "Okay. I guess I'll leave you alone then. Just give me a yell if you need anything, all right?"

"All right. And—" she smiled, "—thank you."

"No need for thanks. You're family now, Michelle."

She closed the door quietly. Michelle stared after her for a long moment. How she wished that Liz's words were true. That she really was a part of this large and warm family. That she and her daughter could be included in these meals, the inside jokes, a part of the intricate support system so evident in their closeness.

She startled herself with the direction of her thoughts. She'd never before considered living outside France, residing in another country where the customs, the language, were so different. Never considered raising her daughter anywhere else. And it was dangerous to be considering it now, because it wasn't an option.

Jake had been acting strangely ever since his run-in with Edgar outside the Evanses' last night. He'd been quiet, thoughtful, almost sad, even. She'd wanted to ask him what was wrong, but hadn't dared. She was afraid of what his answer would be. Had he given up all hope of finding Lili? Had the prospect of coming home, of returning to his normal life, made him realize the mistake he'd made by helping her by marrying her?

She nearly jumped when the door opened again. This time it *was* Jake.

Her heart skipped a beat. If she thought she felt him in the room before, it was nearly overwhelming now. He seemed to fill every inch with his height, his presence.

"Everything okay?" he asked, his eyes dark and watchful.

She nodded. "Yes." She tried for a smile, but couldn't quite conjure one up. Her mind swirled with questions she could no longer ignore, no matter the answers. "No. Everything is not okay." She sank down on the bed and tucked her hair behind her ear. "I think we need to talk."

He nodded slowly. "Yes, I think we do."

She studied his face as she had so often over the past twelve hours, finding nothing there that hadn't been there before, which was precious little. She forced a swallow past her thick throat. "You first."

His small smile surprised her. "You started it."

She closed her eyes, then opened them to stare at the ceiling. "Ever since...after you... I don't know. You've been acting a little strange since last night." She sighed. "I know, everything about this whole thing is—" she gestured helplessly with her hands, "—is strange. But you seem more...distant somehow, not really with me." She searched his eyes. "Is something wrong?"

He didn't say anything. Merely stood looking at her unblinkingly. Then he moved to the bed and sat down stiffly next to her. "Yes, Michelle, something is wrong."

She bit on her bottom lip. She'd known something was wrong, but his admitting it made it all the more real. He was going to tell her he didn't care for her, she knew it. Tell her that he'd been carried away in the heat of passion and that now it was time for them to talk about sending her back to France. If the concept of returning to her home without Lili wasn't bad enough, the thought of going back without hope of ever seeing Jake made her heart break.

"You're sending me back, aren't you?" she said when he didn't speak.

The shocked expression on his face made her heart dip low in her stomach. "What?"

She didn't dare believe that's not what he'd been about to tell her.

"I... Last night, outside Gerald's parents, Edgar..." He looked toward the window. "Is that really what you were worried about?"

She nodded, filled with the urge to touch him, to kiss his endearing mouth. "Edgar what?"

"Edgar told me exactly why you rated such a high priority on the INS hit list."

"Hit list?"

"Those they deem important to get out of the country as soon as humanly possible."

She raised her brows. "I rate that?"

"Uh-huh."

"Why?"

He looked at her again, his gaze probing her face and eyes. God help her, but despite everything going on, she wanted to push him against the mattress and straddle him. "Because of what you did ten years ago in San Francisco."

Every muscle in her body instantly relaxed. She was filled with the sudden, uncontrollable urge to laugh.

13

MICHELLE STOPPED LAUGHING, then her smile quickly faded. Jake's stony expression told her he didn't find the situation the least bit amusing. He was right, of course, considering that Edgar Mollens was still out there somewhere looking for them. Lack of sleep might have been to blame for her foray into hysterics, or the sheer absurdity of the circumstances.

She looked at him a little more closely. "San Francisco? That's the reason I was denied an extension? Why Mollens has been trying to deport me? Because of something I did ten years ago? Something that's hardly worth mentioning?"

His eyes darkened. Apparently he felt differently about the situation, as did his government.

"You're serious, aren't you?"

"Yes, Michelle, I am. Tell me about it."

It took her a minute to call forward the memories in question. It had been so very long since she'd thought, really thought about that time in her life. Yes, right after she'd left the INS office on Monday, she'd considered what had happened in San Francisco a likely reason her extension had been denied. But surely it couldn't have been serious enough to warrant her being placed at the top of the INS hit list.

"What? What should I tell you, Jake?" she asked. "About how I was involved in Blue Earth? That we were against America's underwater testing of nuclear weapons? A group comprised of eighty percent Americans? My God, every college student does the same thing." She looked into her lap.

"Okay, maybe they all didn't join Blue Earth, but most of them wanted to."

"Important papers came up missing while you guys were protesting."

She eyed him. "From where?"

The shadow of suspicion on his face made her cringe. Perhaps this was more serious than she knew. "From the Navy."

"And that's what this is about?"

He didn't answer her.

She pushed from the mattress. She walked from one side of the room to the other, chewing on her fingernail. "That wasn't our mission. We simply went there to stop the U.S.S. *Admiral* nuclear warship from leaving port. Block San Francisco Bay. Focus public attention on their practices via newspaper and television media coverage. At no time was anything said about going on a covert mission to filch any top-secret documents." She began pacing again, trying to think back to that time so long ago. She remembered the salt air, the chilly mornings, though it was the height of summer. The youthful righteousness she'd felt. She remembered also thinking at that time that nothing in her life would be able to equal that moment. A vision of Lili filled her heart and mind as she looked at Jake. Oh, how wrong she had been. That time seemed very long ago, indeed. "The only one I think capable of doing something like that would have been Enrique. The morning of the protest, he disappeared."

"Enrique?"

She recalled the cocky Spaniard in all his arrogant glory. "Enrique Del Jose. He was our second in command, so to speak. He pushed off the boat sometime before dawn. I was the only one on deck, freezing my butt off and wrapped in two wool blankets at the time, waiting to watch the sun rise on the other side of the Golden Gate bridge. He didn't see me, and he seemed startled when I asked him where he was going. He told me he had some sort of business to look after." She stared at Jake. "Wait! It could have been Julie Cochran. She left the boat the night before, claiming she had family in the area, and never made it back until the following day." She looked him squarely in the face. "Or have you ever considered that it wasn't any of us at all, but someone inside who actually stole the documents? I mean, it was a military installation, yes? Wouldn't there have been security up the wazoo?" She leaned her head back and closed her eyes. That argument was neither here nor there. "Anyway, in the impending melee, I never thought about who was missing."

"By melee, you mean the hosing down of the boat, the arrest of nearly everyone on board—"

"Yes." She came to sit next to him, searching his profile. "If the deed was in fact so important, if I was personally suspected of any crime—big or small—because of the group I belonged to, or who I was involved with, why wasn't I detained longer than the others? Tried? Given a jail sentence? Isn't that usually what happens?"

"Involved with?"

Michelle cringed. She had said that, hadn't she? She looked at her hands and the ring on her finger. "Yes. Enrique and I...well, that doesn't matter now, does it?" Never before had she been ashamed of her past, sexual or otherwise. But for some inexplicable reason, she felt reticent to share this information with Jake. Perhaps because she was afraid he'd judge her. Or maybe because none of it mattered anymore. Everything she'd experienced before had been a prelude to meeting him. She forced herself to look at him. "Anyway, wouldn't I have been detained in San Francisco? Taken to trial?"

He stared straight ahead and rubbed the bridge of his nose. "Not normally. If the arrested is a foreign national, procedure usually dictates we send them back home, with a warning to the government in question to keep an eye out for the person. In some cases, the foreign government will actually detain the individual."

Michelle widened her eyes. "You mean France has this on my record, as well?"

He slowly nodded. "Most likely."

"Oh."

"Then you have to combine that information with the fact that when you came this time you flew into Dulles airport, right near the nation's capital."

She stared at him. "You mean it was suspected I'd tried to steal national secrets from D.C.?"

He shrugged, making her hope he found the prospect as stupid as she did.

"I flew into D.C. because this is where Gerald's trip ended. I thought...I thought he had Lili here somewhere."

Finally, his eyes softened. She was filled with the urge to reach out and touch his stalwart face, to trace the ridge of his nose with her thumbs, to drag her fingers along the well-defined lines of his mouth.

"How long were you a member of Blue Earth?"

She sighed and dragged her gaze away from dangerous territory. This is what was keeping her from finding her daughter? "Three months, maybe?" She tucked her hair behind her ear. "Long enough to figure out that for all the philanthropic deeds the group was involved in, the simple fact of it was, to belong, you needed to have money. I..." She bit her bottom lip. "Once I drained the trust fund my mother set up for me, my services were no longer needed." She shrugged. "Not that it mattered to the group. For every poor member they lose, three more wealthy students pop up to take his place." She stared at where a light breeze ruffled the plaid drapes at the window. "God, I haven't thought about that time in my life for a long time."

"Unfortunately it's a fact the U.S. government, or any other government, won't soon forget."

Jake didn't know what to think. He clasped his hands tightly in his lap, mostly to occupy them. He was having a hard time being alone with Michelle in a room with a bed without wanting to climb on top of her, without wanting to forget everything and everyone and claim her all over again. "I've been with the INS for fourteen years, Michelle. Before that, I was in the Marines and I saw... Well, I served overseas. My life has been all about protecting borders, and the importance of doing so. One person. That's all it takes. One zealot who wants a shot at eternal glory, and this entire government could come toppling down. And with it, the world economy." Didn't she understand that? Didn't she understand that her past made her a risk the United States or any other country couldn't afford to take? They didn't care that her daughter had been taken from her, that her intentions were purely noble. All they saw was that she'd been involved in highly questionable activity in the past. One strike and you're out. Given the sheer numbers of foreign nationals applying for visas and green cards from abroad, and the country's vulnerability once a risky individual was within her borders, his job had been to guarantee that those who were out of the game stayed out.

God, his head pounded as though a thousand little hammers were busy building a skyscraper inside his head. What would he have done had he learned this information three days ago, when he'd pumped Brad for information at the INS? Would he have put Michelle on a plane? Would he have seen her as the same risk Edgar did and hunted her down with only one intention?

He didn't know, because the fact remained that he hadn't

known then. He knew she posed no risk at all to the federal government. Her being here didn't jeopardize anyone's life or freedom. The well-being of one particular individual, Lili, his daughter—his stomach dipped—was at risk if Michelle was forced to return to France.

"I see," she said quietly. Her dark eyes held supreme sadness. His throat thickened. What was it about her that made him want to protect her from the world? What magic did she wield over him?

He watched her twist her wedding band around and around. He crooked his index finger under her chin and tilted her head toward him. "No, Michelle, I don't think you do see." She searched his eyes, a spark of hope lighting the depths of hers. "I'm telling you that the situation you're facing is serious. But I'm not bowing out of my promise to you. I told you I'd help you find Lili. And, damn it, I'm going to do that. Because the truth is, when I married you, no matter what the reasons, Lili became just as much my responsibility as yours."

"But—"

"Shh," he said and claimed her mouth with his, not wanting to hear any more questions. Not willing to face the reality that he might have to see through his promise without her here. It all depended on what he could accomplish in the next day or so. And how much time Edgar and the INS were willing to let them have.

He closed his eyes and groaned as he plunged his tongue deep into her mouth.

"SO WHAT, exactly, were you two doing up in your room all morning, Jake?" Connor asked.

Jake stared at his older brother as he, Marc, Mitch, David and Pops all made their way toward their mother's gravesite. The day was warm, the sun nearly at its zenith, dappling the lush grass through thick tree branches.

"It's called none of your damned business," Sean said, and David threw a faux punch in the eldest brother's direction.

Marc snickered. "You'd be amazed how much one can do with the door locked."

"After vows are exchanged," Sean corrected.

Marc's grin widened. "Yeah, well, that's what you think."

Mitch groaned. "Would you guys stop? You'd think we were heading for a bar rather than visiting Mom."

A hush fell over the group as all six came to stand around the simple stone that marked Kathryn Connor McCoy's grave.

"Hard to believe it's been twenty-eight years," Connor said.

Jake didn't respond. Found that he couldn't.

It felt strange being here, honoring a tradition Pops had begun the year following the loss of his wife. He didn't feel as he usually felt. Yes, he supposed he missed her. Rather, he missed the presence of a mother figure in his life. But he no longer mourned her absence as he once had. Other emotions crowded his chest. Additional priorities vied for his attention.

"Wish I could remember more about her," David said, as he did every year.

"Yeah, well, you have trouble remembering the name of the girl you spent last night with. Why should you be expected to remember something from when you were two years old?" Mitch said.

Pops rolled his eyes heavenward, then lay the simple red rose he held across the top of the stone. The rest of them followed suit, until six different types and colors of flowers decorated the top.

"I wasn't with a girl last night," David whispered to

Mitch. "So how am I supposed to remember a name that doesn't exist?"

Mitch narrowed his gaze on the youngest. "Okay, then, the night before."

David's grin nearly swallowed the whole of his face.

"You guys won't be happy until we're all weighed down with a ball and chain," Connor groaned.

"Speaking of ball and chain," Mitch said, "Liz asked to come along today."

Silence fell.

The annual visit had always included only the six of them. It didn't matter where they were, what assignment they were on or what they were doing, they always pulled together for this one day to remember the woman responsible for their walking the earth. Others might overhear their irreverent conversation and question their affection, but it was enough for them to know that this day meant a lot to each of them in their own different ways.

Of course, now that the family had been added to, it was only natural the newer members would want to be included in the visits. Jake didn't find it surprising that Liz had asked to come. And he imagined Mel might want to come, too. He just didn't know how he felt about the concept right about now. Oh, hell, he didn't know how he felt about a whole host of things right about now.

Sean coughed. "I think it's a good idea if we include the girls—"

"Women," Marc and Mitch corrected.

Sean grinned. "Okay, I think it's a good idea if we include the women from here on out." He reached out and touched the top of the stone. "I think your mother would enjoy meeting them. And what with Mel being pregnant, and—" his gaze trailed to Jake "—and with Jake being a dad and all, I think your mother would be glad to see we're all finally moving on."

Was it his imagination, or had his father put a special emphasis on *all*? He glanced at his brothers to find they were all looking at Pops, as well. And Pops was doing his best to keep focused on the headstone.

"So what are you trying to say, Pops?" Connor asked. "What's this 'all' stuff?"

Marc shifted uneasily.

Mitch said, "Come on, we all knew he was involved with someone."

"Correction, we all suspected," Connor said. "You were the only who knew anything."

Mitch shrugged. "That's splitting hairs, isn't it? The fact is, Pops *has* been seeing someone." He glanced at his father. "And it's my guess that it's moved to serious territory." He stuffed his hands in his pockets. "Is that what you're trying to tell us, Pops?"

Sean McCoy seem to turn twenty different shades of red. Jake grimaced. He'd never, ever seen his father blush before. "I wasn't intending to tell you anything." He rubbed the back of his neck, then looked at each one of them in turn. "I mean I was, but not here, not in front of your mother."

"Mom's not really here, Pops," Mitch pointed out.

"And you yourself said she'd probably be glad we were finally moving on," David prompted.

Sean's cheeks expanded as he drew in a long breath. Then he slowly let it out. His gaze seemed especially drawn to Marc, Jake noticed, though he couldn't figure out why. Of the five of them, Marc was the least likely to understand the ins and outs of personal relationships. Okay, maybe Melanie was right, and all the McCoy men were a little deficient in that area, but Marc especially seemed to be lacking.

"The woman I'm seeing...she's... What I mean is..."

Jake grimaced. "I'm coming to learn it's best if you just have out with it."

That roused a laugh from the group. Jake's grimace deepened.

Connor stopped laughing first. "Yeah, Pops, why don't you take your cue from Dr. Spock here and get on with it already?"

"Dr. Spock was a children's specialist," Marc pointed out. "You mean Mr. Spock."

They all stared at Connor.

"So I got it wrong," Connor grumbled.

Sean held up his hands. "Jake's right. There's really no way to say this except to say it." He turned to look squarely at Marc. The middle McCoy appeared shocked at the undivided attention and took a step back. "I've been dating, quite seriously, for a while now." He ran his fingers through his thick, silvery hair. "Aw, hell, Marc, I'm seeing your mother-in-law, Melanie's mom, Wilhemenia Weber."

"What?" Connor asked, his voice a croak.

Jake was surprised, too. But only because he'd thought Pops was going to tell him he was dating someone they all knew from town. In the light of his situation, the information didn't hit him as hard as it seemed to hit his brothers.

He slowly looked them over. From Connor, who pointedly avoided Sean's gaze, to Marc, who stepped backward, then forward again, completely speechless.

Marc finally appeared to gain control over his tongue. "So what you're telling us... What you're saying... Do you mean my mother-in-law may become my stepmother?" he said.

Connor finally looked at Sean as he appeared to work the kinks out of his neck. "Well, you're just going to have to end it."

Jake hiked his brows and watched as Connor turned on his heel and stalked silently away.

MICHELLE SAT at the kitchen table, her fingers wrapped around her mug of black coffee, as Jake's sisters-in-law combined their talents to make dinner. She'd tried to tell them tactfully they'd added far too much salt to the huge roast they'd put into the oven over an hour ago at a temperature sure to char it while leaving the insides raw. But the two women had consulted with each other and decided they'd done the right thing.

She gazed through the back window at the green, green meadows that stretched as far as the eye could see behind the house. Two sleek black stallions—at least, she thought they were stallions—leisurely nibbled at the grass in a nice sized pen while Goliath ran the length of the newly erected wooden fence, barking at the two other males.

Unlike Ohio, this land reminded her somewhat of home. While there were no neat rows of grape vines, there were rolling hills in a shade of green she once thought was only possible in the south of France.

Home.

She supposed she should feel relieved that she still thought of France as home. Because that's exactly what she needed to be thinking about right now. Despite the past few hours spent losing herself in Jake's strong arms, their conversation had made several things very clear. That she had put him at far more risk than she'd thought. And that she needed to go home as soon as possible...for his sake. But before she did so, she had to make sure nothing would happen to him. And, ironically, that meant seeking out the man they had expended so much effort avoiding.

Her heart thudded so hard it hurt.

"What do you think? Should I let them boil for another five minutes?"

Startled from her thoughts, Michelle nearly choked on her coffee when Liz posed the question to a frowning Melanie.

Both women were looking into a large pot they'd filled with potatoes and water, their heads together, emphasizing the difference in their shades of blond. Michelle's gaze drifted to where Mel absently rubbed the small mound that was her stomach. She tried to remember how she'd felt when she'd been six months pregnant with Lili. Her lips twitched in a smile as she remembered all the hopes and dreams that had filled her. All the plans she had made...

Melanie turned from the stove, wiping her hands on a dish towel. "So, Mitch tells us you have a little girl?"

Michelle shouldn't have been surprised by the question, but she was. Of course this family would talk to each other. Just because she thought herself and her problems closed off from the world didn't mean that was the case. She nodded and managed a polite smile. "Yes. Lili. She's...four," she said, keeping things simple. She didn't trust herself to go into detail about how Lili's birthday was this Saturday, and that she would be spending that day away from her. She was afraid she'd end up a blubbering mess.

"That's nice," Mel said, smiling. "You don't mind if I ask you for some advice, do you? I mean, this being my first and all...well, sometimes it gets a little overwhelming, you know?"

Michelle smiled. "Yes. I know."

Fingers of smoke began to billow from the oven door. She'd never seen such an oven before. She suspected the door to the left was for firewood, of all things.

"Oh, no!" Melanie cried, thrusting open the oven door.

The room instantly filled with acrid black smoke.

Michelle got up and pushed open the window. Liz propped open the door. Mel turned first one way, then another, then grabbed a pair of oven mitts and ran the charred meat out the back door. For long minutes, all of them coughed as they grabbed what they could to fan the smoke out. To top everything off, a smoke alarm sounded in the other room.

"Great! Just great!" Melanie said, tossing her oven mitts onto the counter. "You have no idea the big deal Marc is going to make out of this. He's constantly humiliating me in front of our friends—not to mention his family—about my lack of culinary skills. This...well, this one just takes the cake."

"I wouldn't use any food adages right now, Mel." Liz gave a short burst of laughter. Mel glared at her. Liz instantly tried to look contrite, though amusement shone in her bright hazel eyes. "Sorry."

Michelle cleared her throat. "Well, you can always look at it this way. At least they won't ever find out how much salt you put on the meat."

The two women stared at her. Afraid she had said completely the wrong thing, she searched for an excuse to leave the room. Then Mel followed Liz's lead, and laughter chased the last of the smoke from the room.

"Oh, God," Liz said, clutching her side. "That smoke alarm is going to pierce my eardrums."

Mel sighed. "The battery's got to run out sooner or later, right?"

Michelle retrieved the broom from the corner, then led the way into the other room. She positioned the blunt end just so below the alarm. With one calculated whack, the blaring alarm was immediately cut off. She smiled at the two women.

Mel rested both hands against her protruding stomach, her lips twisted in thought. "What is it you said you did for a living again?"

Michelle grasped the broom tightly. They hadn't exactly gotten around to sharing information such as what each of them did in their daily lives. "I'm, um, a chef."

Liz smacked her hand against her forehead. "God, do I ever feel dense."

Mel linked her arm with Michelle's. "Well, why didn't you say something before?" she asked as she led the way to the kitchen.

Liz took her other arm. "Maybe because we were too busy acting like Southern know-it-alls."

Michelle had spent the past hour reviewing ways she might be able to put together a meal with the salvageable remains of the other women's attempts. She smiled as Mel and Liz released her.

"Just tell us what you want us to do," Mel said.

And Michelle did.

JAKE STARED at his plate in barely disguised shock. This couldn't be dinner. Where was the thick slab of meat? The mountain of potatoes dripping with butter and gravy? He turned again to see the bread on a small plate at his left elbow, then looked at Michelle. She seemed to be purposely avoiding his gaze. He frowned, then looked around the table, seeing that everyone had the same thing he had.

In the center of the large plates that usually held piles of food was one perfect, silver-dollar-sized circle of what appeared to be beef—though he couldn't be sure because some sort of white sauce covered it—with what looked like a boiled potato decorated with—were those parsley leaves?—next to it. A small helping of cut green beans tossed with some sort of sliced nuts was to the right. And some sort of brown sauce had been dribbled over the plate in a kind of zigzag design.

If he thought the McCoy men had been quiet before, they were downright silent now. Nobody messed with their meat and potatoes.

"It's bourguignonne and *pomme de terre*," Michelle said quietly. "I hope you like it."

Jake heard what sounded like a snicker from Liz. He caught Michelle biting her bottom lip to keep from laughing, as well. What were they up to?

"This the first course?" Marc said, looking hopefully at the stove and countertops. Both were empty of a solitary pan. "I hope this is the first course." He forked his potato. "This had better be the first course. Oww!"

Mel lifted her fork, then smiled at everyone.

Sean cleared his throat. "Well, Michelle, this looks...pretty enough to frame."

"You're supposed to eat food, not frame it," Connor grumbled from the other end of the table.

Jake looked back and forth between the two men. He'd hoped that during the drive from the cemetery to the house, things would have cooled down enough for them to have reached some sort of truce. But the interior of Mitch's new four-door truck had remained awfully quiet. Not even David's half-assed attempts at humor had been able to crack the silence.

Mitch was the first to try the mystery meat. At the sound of his silverware against the plate, the occupants of the table watched as he carefully cut off a small bite, then slowly put it into his mouth. One chew. Two. Then he closed his eyes and made a humming sound Jake had never heard from him before. "Oh, Michelle. This is... What I mean is...wow. That's the best piece of meat I've ever tasted."

"Piece of meat? Scrap is more like it," Connor said under his breath as David and Jake tried the food.

The explosion of flavor on his tongue was unlike anything Jake had ever experienced. He reluctantly swallowed the bite, then looked at Michelle. She was concentrating a little too fully on her plate.

Mitch leaned closer to his wife and lowered his voice, though everyone in the room heard him anyway. "Liz, what happened to that big roast I saw in the refrigerator this morning?"

Liz smiled a little too widely. "This is it."

Sean coughed and reached for his glass of milk. "You cook much, Michelle?"

Jake wiped his mouth with his napkin. "Actually, Michelle's a chef."

David brightened. "I knew this food looked familiar. I went to this frou—um, this French place in D.C. last spring. The stuff they served looked just like this. Huge plate... Anyway, I've gotta tell you the cost of the meal would have been enough for me to eat off for a month. So I guess we should feel honored to have a chef of Michelle's caliber in our midst."

This time Michelle tittered in a way that shocked Jake. She lifted her napkin to her mouth but didn't look at him. "Um, pardon me."

The go-ahead on the food having been given, it took a whole two minutes for the contents of the plates to vanish, not even leaving the decorative design as the men sopped it up with their bread. Thank God there was at least a lot of that.

"Well," Marc said, "I think I speak for everyone when I say that was certainly a meal to remember." He began to push from the table.

"I second that." David followed suit.

Mitch cleared his throat. "Um, Michelle? While I enjoyed the meal and everything, the next time around...you may want to double, no, quadruple, the portion size. We McCoy men really cut loose come meal time. And meat—a lot of it— and mashed potatoes hits the spot unlike anything else."

Jake could have sworn that was a smile Michelle hid behind her napkin. "I'll keep that in mind, Mitch. Thank you."

Liz sat up straighter. "I, for one, thoroughly enjoyed the meal, Michelle. Feel free to cook for us any time you want."

Jake couldn't figure out what was going on, but the way the three women eyed each other, then quickly looked away told him something certainly was.

Near the door to the living room, he caught David whispering to Marc, "You put up the money for the pizza, and I'll run into Culpepper to get it."

"Make it two pizzas with the works, and you've got yourself a deal," Marc said.

A moment later, the sound of a football game filled the interior of the house, another tradition now that autumn was just around the corner.

Michelle began to clear the plates with Liz and Mel, leaving Jake, Connor and Pops at the table.

"We'll get those," Pops said, taking the small stack Michelle had gathered. "It's only fair seeing as you gals took care of the food."

Connor snorted. Jake glared at him and took the glasses to the sink. Connor pushed from the table then stalked through the back door.

"What's that all about?" Mel asked, putting a fresh pot of coffee on to brew.

Liz emptied a bag of store-bought cookies onto a plate, stuck one in her mouth, then placed the plate on the table along with clean glasses and a gallon of milk. "You know, now that you mention it, all you guys were a little quiet during dinner. Did something happen?"

Sean met Jake's gaze. "Nothing that won't blow over in a day or two."

The phone rang. Pops snatched the receiver up in the middle of the second ring. He glanced at Jake, then rounded the corner, apparently in a bid to speak in private. To Mel's mom, Wilhemenia? Jake didn't know. But one thing was for sure—nothing would blow over if Sean didn't let things lie for a bit. Connor was more upset than Jake had ever seen him. It was a good sign that he'd stuck around for dinner, but Jake guessed that was more to see how their father would ultimately respond to what he'd said than an indication that Connor's mood had improved.

He glanced at Melanie, wondering what she'd have to say when she found out what had really gone down at the cemetery that morning.

"Coming through!" Jake moved out of the way as David zipped through the room, undoubtedly on his way to pick up the pizza.

In the chaos of his family's constantly industrious lives, Jake almost forgot how Michelle had avoided looking directly at him during dinner. Almost. He sought her out, only to find her stacking dishes in the dishwasher, her back firmly to him. He didn't know what had happened while he was gone, but he was sure it was more than the dinner they'd just eaten.

14

MICHELLE CLOSED the bedroom door with a soft click. She'd told Jake she really needed to get some sleep. She did, but that's not the reason she wanted to be alone. Dinner may have been all fun and games for her, Mel and Liz, but there was nothing fun about what she needed to do now.

She sank down on the single bed and wrapped her arms around herself to gather warmth, despite the heat of the day. What would Jake's family say if they knew about her past? Jake had seemed more upset by the news than she would have thought possible. And he knew her better than the others. Cared for her more.

She stared at the cell phone on the bed in front of her. She reached for it, then pulled her hand back.

Coward, she told herself.

Yes, she admitted, she was a coward and a fool. A grade-A fool for thinking that this thing with Jake could have ended any other way than it had to.

She rubbed her forehead. How easy it was when enfolded in Jake's strong arms to believe everything would be all right. That somehow he could move the mountains that separated her from her daughter, and protect her from his government, who wanted to send her back to France.

She wasn't sure when this had all happened. She suspected way back in the beginning after the purse snatching, when he'd played knight in shining armor to her damsel in distress. She'd taken one look at those sober gray eyes, those

large hands, and all that deeply suppressed need for someone to share the burden with had bubbled to the surface. She
rolled her eyes to stare at the ceiling. Who was she kidding?
She'd wanted to shift the leaden weight on her shoulders
completely over to him. Trouble was, he'd been more than
willing to accept the load. Some new millennium woman she
was.

Still, it baffled her how, after spending twenty-eight years
on her own, having and raising her daughter, forging a career and a life for herself, how she'd managed to get sucked
into visions of a fairy-tale life she'd stopped believing in long
ago.

But none of that changed that all possibility of finding Lili
was exhausted. And that by staying here, without taking any
action, she was only delaying the inevitable. While that had
appealed to her a mere hour before...well, now she recognized the unfairness of it.

Already, she'd begun to make her niche in his family. Liz
and Mel—they were the sisters she'd always hoped her step-
sisters would be but never were. They were happy and witty
and incredibly smart, and she knew that it wouldn't take
very long to come to care for them—and the rest of the Mc-
Coy bunch—very much. Just as she'd come to care immea-
surably for Jake. By allowing those bonds to grow stronger,
she'd be hurting more than just Jake. And the pain she
would feel would only deepen.

God, when had the world gotten so damned complicated?
Since when was it a sin to play the role of rebellious college
student? To want her daughter back with her mother where
she belonged? When had it become a bad thing to love someone so much you would sacrifice even your own heart for
them?

She reached into her backpack and rustled around. Frowning, she began taking the things out one by one. After a thor-

ough search, it became apparent she was short one small stuffed elephant.

She closed her eyes. Lili would have a fit.

Oh, dear, sweet Lili...

She didn't know how she would possibly live without her daughter for one more day, much less the years that yawned before her. One thing was plain, though. She would never give up looking for her. Never. She would have to do it from France. She didn't care where she'd find the money for it. She'd beg, borrow and steal, work three jobs, borrow from her father, to get it. Whatever it took. But she would never stop looking, no matter how old she or her daughter got. She only hoped that one day Lili would forgive her for not having been a better mother.

Her fingers circled the cold plastic of the cell phone. After spreading out her visa papers, she carefully punched in the contact number, then lifted the phone to her ear. "Agent Edgar Mollens, please."

THE STUFFED ELEPHANT looked ridiculously fragile in his large hands. Jake ran his thumbs down the length of the rounded belly, then fixed the lopsided trunk. He'd never been much for toys when he was a kid. That this one could hold so much significance baffled him. But it did.

He slid a glance toward the stairs Michelle had disappeared up a half hour ago, claiming a need for some major shut-eye, then he looked at his brothers. Two large pizza boxes sporting nothing but goo littered the coffee table, and every other available piece of furniture sported McCoy males in various stages of repose. The football game was at half time, Liz and Mel sat in the kitchen discussing recipes Michelle had passed on to them, Pops was in the hall on the phone again and Connor's absence was obvious but not mentioned.

He still didn't know exactly what had happened at dinner, but he was sure the acrid smell of something burned had more to do with the lack of meat than Michelle's cooking skills. What had warmed him was the way Michelle was getting along so well with his sisters-in-law. Hell, he wasn't as comfortable around them, and he'd had months to adjust, while all she had needed was a couple hours. He shook his head, deciding it was a woman thing.

He wasn't sure when it had happened, or why. But an overwhelming urge to make her his wife for real, for always, filled him to the point of pain. The impulse could have begun as early as the day they met, when he'd sat across that café table from her, watching her lick foam from her upper lip. Or when he'd brought her home, mingling reality with the surreal quality of the past few days until he could no longer discern one from the other. He couldn't imagine his life without her in it. Tucking her tumble of dark hair behind her ear. Smiling her sexy little smile. Getting him to bare his deepest emotions in a way that scared the hell out of him, yet made him feel...real.

The memory of the quick ceremony in Toledo, Ohio, emerged. He cringed. She deserved better than a few hastily exchanged vows before a judge with a drunken pastor as their witness. As cutting edge as Michelle appeared to be, she'd wanted a traditional wedding with all the trappings, and he found he wanted to give it to her. The whole nine yards. The wedding dress with a train that would stretch all the way to France, if that's what she wanted. A full bridal court. A huge rock that could try but fail to match the light that seemed to make her glow from within.

He glanced longingly at the stairs. What he wouldn't give to go up to his room and climb into that bed next to Michelle. And then propose to her properly.

But he couldn't, not yet. This time he intended to do it right, but he had some things to do first.

Jake stuck the elephant on the chair behind him then cleared his throat. "Guys, this is, um, a little difficult for me, but..."

Marc was practically one with the sofa, his long legs stretched out next to the pizza boxes. He regarded Jake with a long look, then crossed his arms. "Gotta tell you, Jake, we were wondering when you were going to get around to asking."

Mitch cleared his throat from Pops's arm chair. Jake blinked at him, not missing the grin he threw his way. "Anyone time it?"

David made a production of looking at his watch. "Nine hours, twenty minutes and thirty seconds." He grimaced. "Shoot. That means Pops won."

Jake rubbed his palms on his sweats. Sweats. He still couldn't believe he was wearing them. Truth was, the suckers were mighty comfortable. "Anyone feel like catching me up to speed? Ask what? And what did Pops win?"

David sat forward, resting his forearms on his jeans-clad knees. "Well, ask us to help you find little Lili, of course."

Marc took his feet off the table. "We all bet how long it would take for you to finally speak up. Pops won."

Jake rubbed his chin, realizing he needed a shave. "What?"

David grinned. "Truth is, while you were upstairs this morning, doing whatever it is you were doing with Michelle, we all took turns with the phone and started pulling strings and yanking chains. We would have filled you in before, but we were waiting for any real news. Besides, we figured you'd ask for help eventually, and we didn't want you to think we were interfering by bringing up the idea first."

Jake frowned, trying to take in what his brothers were saying but feeling as though he was missing a few of the finer points.

Mitch's face sobered. "Granted, during our phone conversations two days ago, you didn't give me a whole hell of a lot to go on. But it was enough to piece together the situation. And with that slime puppy Mollens calling here—"

Jake nearly choked. "Edgar Mollens called here?"

"Yeah. Got Pops first. It wasn't pretty," Marc answered. "He tried back again yesterday, but didn't get much farther with Mitch."

Mitch shrugged. "Shoot me, but I don't like people threatening me or any of my brothers."

"What did he say?"

"Nothing that matters now." Mitch waved him off. "What I'm trying to say is that about an hour ago, Gerald Evans, Lili's father, was pulled in by authorities in his area, and we're awaiting further word. Pops's doing, if you want to know. While I still have some contacts at the FBI, no one was willing to do anything quite this shady."

David spoke. "Hey, I have some pull with the DCPD, too, you know. It wasn't just Pops."

Three McCoy brothers stared at him.

Marc shrugged. "Unfortunately, I wasn't able to do much with the Secret Service, either—"

Jake held his hands up. "Whoa, whoa, whoa. What are you guys telling me here? That you went ahead and worked on finding Lili on your own? Without being asked? Without..." His voice trailed off, the explosion of gratitude he felt for these brothers of his overwhelming in its intensity. For the first time in a day, hope surged through his veins, joining his increasing determination to find Michelle's...their daughter.

"Yes, that's exactly what we're saying." The perpetual

grin that split David's face vanished, replaced by a weightier expression, one Jake had never seen him wear before.

Pops came into the room from the kitchen, apparently having finished his telephone conversation. Liz and Mel were on either side of him, their confusion evident. The recliner creaked as Mitch got up. "In fact, I'm betting Pops has some news to share."

Jake practically leaped from his chair. He looked toward the stairs to find Michelle standing near the bottom, leaning against the wall, listening. Myriad emotions flickered across her features, her eyes large in her pale face. He wanted to go to her, but he could do little more than stand there and stare at her, then Pops, his heart thudding in his chest.

"I've found her," Sean announced.

The expectant hush that filled the room was nearly suffocating. Jake stepped forward. Michelle rushed to Sean. "Where? How? Can I see her?"

Pops's grin was all-consuming. "She's at a downtown D.C. hotel with her grandparents. How? Well, that's a little more complicated." He reached out and touched Michelle's arm. "And, yes, you can go see her. In fact, you can pick her up as soon as you're ready."

The floor shifted beneath Jake's feet. It seemed impossible that after everything they'd done, everywhere he and Michelle had gone, his father had accomplished in a few hours what they couldn't in several days. "Uncomplicate things, Pops. Explain to me how...how you found her."

Sean's grin melted into a simple smile. "I'd really like to take all the credit for this, but I can't. You'll see what I mean." He cleared his throat. "This morning I had a few of my buddies at the station call a few of their buddies, until someone found someone who worked in the Lucas County sheriff's office in northwest Ohio. It didn't take much convincing to have them pick up one Gerald Evans and take him to the local station. It was there under pressure of questioning that he revealed where his parents were." He crossed his arms. "The funny thing is, Lili's grandparents had already come to the conclusion that what they were doing was wrong, no matter that the law was on their side, technically speaking. They were already on their way to D.C. from where they were staying in New Hampshire—" his gaze scanned Michelle's ashen face "—to bring little Lili back to you, Michelle. They checked into a hotel a short time ago and are waiting for you to come."

Michelle looked ready to rush out the door. Sean gently grasped her shoulders.

"One more thing. They, the Evanses, asked me to pass on their apologies—"

"You've seen them?" Jake interjected.

"No. I spoke with them on the phone. I wanted to make sure everything was on the up-and-up before I said anything." He looked at Michelle. "Anyway, once everything is settled, they said they'd like to be in contact with you, you know, to keep them posted on how Lili is doing. And while they'd understand if you said no, they'd like you to consider allowing Lili to come visit every now and again."

He handed Michelle a slip of paper. "That's their number. Sometime down the line, you might want to give them a call, you know, when you're ready. Or—" he shrugged "—don't. I figure after what they've done, I wouldn't blame you if you didn't want your daughter to see them again, even if they do gain some points for bringing her back to you."

"Which hotel?" Jake asked, grasping the item he'd left on the chair and checking for his car keys.

Sean told him.

Jake took Michelle's arm and led her toward the kitchen.

"Hey, wait up!" Marc called, following.

"You're not going anywhere without me," David said.

Liz dabbed at her eyes. "Mitch, warm up the truck. We're going to need the room."

MICHELLE COULDN'T quite bring herself to trust that her daughter had really been found. She stood in the hotel lobby shaking like a hand mixer, expecting any moment to hear that the Evanses had changed their minds and checked out, no forwarding address provided. Or to be told that she could see Lili, but Sean had misunderstood and that her daughter was going to remain with her grandparents.

Jake's presence next to her meant more than she could express, but she didn't dare turn to him for support or seek warmth in his arms. No matter what happened in the next few minutes, she'd made her decision. There was no going back now.

The elevator doors dinged then slowly slid open. Michelle's heart nearly burst straight through her chest.

Lili!

Inside the cubicle, her daughter held the hands of Gerald's parents and had her little chin tilted up, rattling on about something or other, so she didn't see Michelle right away. Then she shifted to look into the lobby. She stopped speaking mid-sentence, then catapulted herself toward Michelle.

"Maman! Maman!"

Michelle's sob seemed to fill every corner of the lobby...and seep through every crack in Jake's heart.

He stood silently and watched as Lili flew into her mother's arms, speaking in a combination of rapid-fire English and French, her small arms squeezing Michelle's neck, her short skirt hiking up to reveal cartoon-laden undies.

"I know you tried to call, baby," Michelle murmured, covering her daughter's face with kisses and tears. She must have realized she'd spoken in English, because she immediately started speaking in French.

Pops came to stand next to Jake while the rest of the Mc-Coy bunch hung back. It had taken three cars to get them all there, but Jake was glad they had come. "Pretty little thing, isn't she?" Pops said.

Jake nodded, completely incapable of speech. Not because he didn't have anything to say, which had always been the case not long ago. But because he couldn't possibly push anything past his throat if he tried.

"I always thought French was one of the more interesting languages," Mitch said from the other side of Jake. "Do you know what they're saying?"

Jake shook his head.

Behind him, Marc loudly blew his nose into a tissue. Right on the heels was David's voice "For cripe's sakes, are you crying? Jaysus, Marc! What is it with you married guys, anyway? Before you know it, you're going to be crying at those TV commercials like Mel and Liz do."

"Stuff a sock in it, David," Mel said, taking the tissue from Marc and sopping the tears from her cheeks.

Jake listened to the arguments with half an ear. His focus was on the woman he loved, who was being reunited with her daughter. And he was standing across the room completely paralyzed, without a clue as to what he should do, if he should be doing anything at all.

He was also aware of the prickle of exclusion. As much as he hated to admit it, he recognized the sensation too well to ignore it. It was the same way he'd felt growing up. He'd always been a part of the McCoy family. Participated in the Sunday dinners. Visited at least twice, if not three times a week. But he'd never really felt...included. That is, until today, when his brothers and father had pitched in without even being asked to do something for him. Just because he was one of them. He'd realized then that he didn't have to tow it alone any longer. That he'd never had to.

He also stumbled onto the true, mind-boggling extent of his feelings for Michelle.

When had he stopped being a silent loner? When had he trusted himself and those he talked to with things he had to say—without fear that they'd ridicule him or that he'd embarrass himself?

He knew exactly when that moment had happened. The instant he met and fell in love with Michelle Lambert. Opened his heart and let her in, not just partially, but all the way.

He noticed that Connor had joined the group at some point in the chaos of leaving the house and had come along. He stood to the side, his arms crossed, his gaze hooded as he watched the reunion. Of all of them, he seemed the least impressed with what was going on.

Michelle finally disentangled her arms from around her daughter, though she kept a grip on her, as if afraid the girl would vanish again if she completely let her go. She turned her daughter so that they faced Jake. She looked at him and said something into Lili's ear in French. Then she smiled and repeated it in English. "Lili, honey, say hello to Jake."

Lili hesitated. Her gaze seemed locked on his knees as she put one of her shoes on top of the other. Then she looked into Jake's face.

Jake swallowed so hard, he could swear it echoed through the room. "Hello, Lili," he managed to say.

She gazed at him intently a moment, and in that instant Jake realized how very much she resembled her mother. "Hello."

Jake's heart did a funny little somersault in his chest. His gaze flicked to Michelle. But rather than looking at him, she was saying something to Lili in French, her face serious. "Nice to meet you, Mr. McCoy," Lili said slowly.

"It's...nice to meet you, too, Lili," he said, trying to keep emotion from his voice. "I, um, have someone here who's been looking forward to seeing you." He produced the stuffed elephant from behind his back.

"Julianne!" Lili practically flew to him.

Jake crouched, holding the toy out to her. His gaze swept her from the tip of her blond head to her toes. She was so small. So fragile. He wanted to reach out and touch her, but didn't dare. He contented himself with a smile. A smile she returned before she stepped back to her mother, murmuring in French to her inanimate friend.

"Thank you," Michelle said quietly, though she could have been talking to anyone given the way she looked strictly at Lili.

Jake wasn't sure what was happening. Why had Michelle instructed Lili to call him Mr. McCoy rather than Jake? But now that he had put a name to the feeling he'd grown to know too well, the rejection he felt cut deeper than it had.

Michelle rose to her full height, clasping Lili's hand in both of hers. "I…I don't know what to say," she said to the group, biting her lip as her eyes filled with tears anew. She included the Evanses, who stood just outside the elevator, in her sweep. "Thank you…thank you all so very much."

A couple of Jake's brothers coughed, and behind him, Marc blew his nose again.

Lili tugged on Michelle's hand. Michelle bent to let her daughter say something in her ear. The stage whisper ended up being louder than regular conversation. "I love Nana and Grandpa, *Maman*. And they love me."

Michelle seemed to choke on her reply as she smoothed wisps of Lili's white-blond hair from her face. "I know, baby. I know."

Her gaze lifted again to Pops and the rest of them. Jake tried to tell himself it was the emotion of the moment, that with all that was going on Michelle was preoccupied, but again he got the distinct impression she was purposely avoiding his gaze. "I don't know how I'm ever going to repay you. But I will." She finally looked at him, and the finality he saw there nearly booted his heart straight from his chest. "I will."

TWO HOURS LATER, Jake stood outside his bedroom door, his eyes tightly closed, his hand a hairbreadth away from knocking on the hard wood. He released his breath.

The long drive to the McCoy place from D.C. had been bad enough, what with Liz, Melanie and Pops riding with him and Michelle and a very chatty Lili, who seemed to bask in all the attention, none the worse for wear after her ordeal. But as soon as they were inside the house, Michelle had all but swept little Lili up and disappeared into his bedroom, where they'd been for the past half hour.

"English, *Maman*. I want to talk English," he heard Lili say through the door.

There was a pause, then Michelle said, "All right, baby. We'll speak English, if that's what you'd like. Come here." The sound of clothes rustling. Jake envisioned her pulling Lili onto her lap. "I'm so very, very proud of you, do you know that? So very proud."

The girl giggled.

"And I missed you so very, very much."

"How much?"

Jake smiled where he stood on the other side of the door. It appeared Lili shared more in common with her mother than her knockout good looks.

"More than the whole wide world, baby," Michelle said and loudly kissed her. "More than the whole wide world."

Jake opened his hand from where it was rolled into a fist, debating whether he should interrupt. Truth was, he didn't know where things stood between him and Michelle. Now that she had her daughter back, was there room in her heart for him?

The door opened. Jake started, looking guiltily at Michelle, who appeared to be just as surprised to find him there.

He cleared his throat. "I'm sorry...I just wanted to make sure that...you know, everything is okay."

The smile she gave him was tremulous, at best. "Yes. Everything is more than okay, Jake."

He scanned her rosy features, thinking he would never tire of looking at her. Drinking in her energy. Her innate sensuality.

Then her gaze slid to the floor, and she opened the door a little farther. "Come in. I was just coming to get you."

Uh-oh. Jake stood frozen for a long moment, not liking the sound of her voice, the way she had said the words. He reluctantly followed her in and closed the door behind him.

Lili sat at his desk, her thumb firmly in her mouth, her elephant sitting in front of her. "Hi, Mr. McCoy," she said around her thumb.

There was that funny little weightlessness again mixed with grim apprehension. He smiled. "Hi again, Lili."

Michelle crossed her arms and nodded toward the bed. "Please...sit down."

Jake slowly did as she requested, his gaze glued to the little girl playing with her toy.

"I...I really don't know where to start, Jake."

"The beginning is as good a place as any," he said quietly, finally dragging his attention away from the little girl to her mother.

"Okay..." She sat on the bed, too, well away from him. "I can't tell you how very grateful I am for all you've done for me...and for Lili...."

What was she saying? She didn't have to thank him. They were a family. His chest tightened. Weren't they?

"I know how much you've put on the line to help me. To help us. I..." She sucked her bottom lip into her mouth. "I just want you to know that I won't be causing you problems anymore."

He sat there for a long moment, feeling as if the room were spinning out of control. His entire line of sight narrowed in on her. Only her.

"What...what are you saying?"

"I...what I mean to say is, Lili...we'll be going into the city today. Catching a flight back to France tomorrow morning."

Her words didn't sink in on the first go-round. He stared at her mouth, trying to verify that it had indeed moved...had really said what he thought it had. Michelle's unwavering sober expression told him it had.

He sprung from the bed so quickly, he nearly catapulted her off the other side. "What?"

"Please," she said quickly, rising from the bed and rounding it to face him. Her fingers felt warm and dry where she caressed the side of his face. "Please, don't make this any harder than it already is. I've caused enough trouble for you, Jake. You said yourself that your government will never be able to overlook my past. They'll never let me stay here." She blinked away the wetness filling her soft brown eyes. "And you..." Her smile was sweetly sad. "I can't see you anywhere else but here." She shrugged in a gesture of frustration. "Can't you see this is the only way? That my leaving is the only possible outcome? We've been fooling ourselves if we thought it could work out differently. It can't—"

"It can," he said vehemently, gently grasping her upper arms and hauling her closer. "Michelle, please listen to me. I..." He hesitated at the slight shaking of her head. "Look, I've never been great with words. Lord knows I'm far from a poet, but we can work this out, together. We can go before the immigration review board, hell, court if we have to. My clean record can cancel out yours if it comes down to it."

The shaking of her head grew more decisive. "I can't... won't let you do that, Jake."

"Isn't that my decision to make?"

"That's just it, isn't it? Every decision that's been made since I met you has been your decision. This one has to be mine."

He found it nearly impossible to draw a breath. His heart thudded like a bass drum in his chest; fear threaded through his bloodstream like a poison. "Early on, before we...before we became a couple, you said something to me that really hit home. You said all you wanted was to find Lili—" he motioned toward the little girl who had laid her head against the desktop and was drifting to sleep "—and go home. Go back to the way your life was before all this started." His throat grew unbearably tight. "I remember sitting there looking at you, marveling over the feelings starting to grow even then, thinking that I was just waiting for my life to begin." He searched her eyes. "Don't you see, up until that point, I didn't know my life was missing anything. Not until I met you. I..." His throat made a clicking sound as he swallowed. "I love you, Michelle. And I want you and Lili to stay. To be my family."

He stood there for long moments, frozen. He'd never told anyone before that he loved them. Never bared his soul the way he had just bared it to Michelle. Hell, he hadn't even known he possessed a soul until she had touched it. But there it was. And he'd never felt so naked in his life.

She averted her gaze. "I love you, too, Jake."

Her voice was so low it was almost a whisper. But far from being the happy proclamation he might have wished it to be, it seemed a sad punctuation point. He watched her bite her lip, presumably to keep the tears welling in her eyes from trickling down her cheeks. "But it's too late."

There was a brief knock at the door. Jake moved to tell whoever it was to go the hell away, but Michelle placed a finger over his lips. "Yes?"

The door opened a couple of inches. "I'm sorry to interrupt," Liz said quietly, her gaze darting everywhere but to their faces. "But if we're going to make it...well, we're going to have to leave in the next few minutes."

"Okay," Michelle whispered.

Liz hesitated. "You want me to take Lili downstairs to wait with me?"

Michelle nodded, her gaze steadfastly on Jake's.

A sleepy Lili easily took Liz's hand and was led from the room. The click of the door catch was unusually loud in the quiet room.

Jake opened his mouth, trying to work it around words that made sense.

"Shh," Michelle whispered, sliding into his embrace.

Jake stood, not daring to touch her, groaning when he felt the hard thud of her heart beating through her rib cage.

"I just want you to know that I..." Her words trailed off, her voice catching.

Jake pulled back to look into her face.

"I want you to know that our time together...it was the best of my life. The love I feel for you...it will never go away. I will carry it with me always." She let him go.

Jake felt as if the very ground had been snatched out from under his feet.

Michelle twisted the simple gold band on her finger. She opened his hand and slowly placed the hot band of metal in his palm, then closed his fingers over it.

Then she was gone.

15

JAKE FELT LIKE breaking something. He wanted to take a baseball bat and pound something, anything into a pulp. Make it resemble the mess that was his life as he watched Liz back out of the drive with Michelle, little Lili waving at him through the back window.

He didn't understand a thing. Despite all Michelle's explaining, a thousand and one questions remained. *She loved him.* His heart skipped a beat. *She didn't want to stay.* His heart dropped to the ground where surely someone would come by and stomp on it any second.

The first person who came up was Pops.

"Did they decide some shopping was in order?"

The fact that someone had spoken took forever to register as Jake watched Liz's car disappear from view. It took a few moments longer for the words to make any sense.

"What?"

He turned to find Pops standing next to him. "I asked if the girls decided some shopping was in order, you know, for little Lili."

"Shopping?"

Pops's grin faded from his lined face. "Jake? Where are they going?"

Jake turned and went into the house, stalking the length of it, then pacing back. When he came to a stop, Pops was just where he'd left him.

"You know, I thought finding Lili...by reuniting Michelle

with her daughter, that the three of you could start being a family."

"Family? There's not going to be any family, Pops. Liz is taking Michelle and Lili into town so they can catch a flight out to France."

"What?" It was Pops's turn to look as though someone had just sucker punched him.

"I said—"

"I heard what you just said, Jake. I'm just having trouble believing it." His chest puffed out as he took a deep breath. "You know, I thought this day couldn't possibly get any worse. First, the thing at your mom's gravesite, with Connor saying what he did, then my having to decide to break things off with Billie—"

Jake held up his hand. "Whoa. Wait a minute. You're going a little too fast for me here." This communicating stuff was going to take a little longer to get used to. Then again, he was tempted to never speak again. Look at where his opening up had gotten him.

He squinted at his father. "Did you just say you broke things off with Mel's mother?"

Sean looked over his shoulder, relief washing over his face, apparently because Melanie wasn't anywhere near. "Yeah. She wasn't too happy about it, either. I mean, she didn't say anything—which is how I knew she wasn't happy. Just kind of made this *oh* sound. You know the kind. That small word that says so much yet so little?"

Jake frowned. No, he didn't know.

"Anyway, I just want to ask you one thing, Jacob William McCoy... Are you *crazy*? I mean, have you completely lost your mind?" He pointed a finger in the direction the car had gone. "Your brothers and I didn't go to all that trouble just so you could blithely wave as those two women leave your life.

And I sure as hell know that *you* didn't go through what you have over the past few days toward that end, either."

Jake stared at him mutely.

Sean paced a short way, then stalked back, his eyes blazing. "What is it with you boys, anyway? I mean, I know I haven't always been a good father, that my parenting skills were pretty much nonexistent while you guys were growing up. But, good Lord, you all couldn't be any dumber had I purposely set out to make you that way."

Jake blinked at him, completely dumbstruck.

"Well, don't just stand there, you idiot! Go and bring them back!"

He couldn't move. Then, finally, he found himself shaking his head. "You don't understand, Pops. I didn't let them go anywhere. Michelle just...well, she just up and left. Going after her isn't going to accomplish anything."

"How can you be so sure?"

"Because she made me that way."

Sean looked at him long and hard, then turned and walked into the house, the screen door slapping closed behind him.

"MEET ME *at the diner in downtown Manchester.*"

Edgar Mollens's final words echoed through Michelle's mind as she slowly slid into the red booth and anxiously glanced around the retro-style diner called Bo and Ruth's Paradise Diner.

"Look, *Maman!* An angel." She absently watched as Lili plucked a candied cherub from a perch in the middle of the table.

"Yes, *ma cherie,* an angel," she said, not having the energy to correct her. She feared the image of Jake's crushed expression was burned into her mind forever. She saw the haunted shadow in his eyes whenever she closed her own. She felt her heart break all over again at the memory of his speechless countenance, his obvious pain.

Liz slid in across from her, her eyes watchful, her posture unsure. A wiry-haired waitress sashayed up to the booth and regarded Liz with a wide smile. "Well, if it isn't the little newlywed come to town for a visit."

Michelle's gaze was riveted to the woman's face. She wondered how many people knew of her and Jake's...arrangement. She didn't dare call it a marriage. Not now. It was too dangerous to her mental health to think of their time together as anything more than an almost was.

Liz coughed. "Mitch and I have been married a whole two months now, Myra. I hardly think that qualifies as newlyweds."

Michelle felt her cheeks go hot. Of course. The woman Liz had called Myra wasn't referring to her; she was talking about Liz.

"And who do we have here?" Myra asked.

"I'm Lili," Michelle's daughter announced.

"Well, hello there, little Lili. I'm Myra. And do I ever have just the thing for you."

"Ice cream!" Lili exclaimed.

Michelle watched her daughter as if from a distance. While much remained the same, in the two hours since they had been reunited, she'd come to notice certain changes, both subtle and obvious. The closest she could come to describing it was that her daughter had undergone a certain type of Americanization in the two months since Gerald had taken her from France. Her English, while accented, was clear. Her behavior was decidedly more outgoing. And she bore no obvious emotional scars from her ordeal.

Tears welled in her eyes as she counted her blessings.

She reached out to touch her daughter's hair, but Lili

pushed her hand away as she introduced the angel to her stuffed elephant, Julianne.

Michelle's gaze trailed through the window to the street. Was Edgar already there somewhere, watching them?

Myra served Lili a child-size portion of cherry pie complete with ice cream, then poured coffee for Michelle and Liz. After a few failed attempts at striking up a conversation with what must have seemed to her a morose pair, the waitress shrugged her skinny shoulders and sashayed behind the main counter, where Michelle noticed two beefy men holding coffee cups and openly watching them from their stools. Through the window that looked into the kitchen, a man wearing a white knit cap and another woman also looked on.

Liz took a long pull from her cup. "Look, Michelle...I know I promised I wouldn't ask any unwelcome questions, but..." She sighed, then sat back in the booth. "I'm going to have to break that promise. Are you sure you know what you're doing?"

Michelle stared into her cup, trying not to compare her romantic future to the murky black liquid. She slowly nodded. "Yes. It is the only way to guarantee Jake won't get into trouble."

Liz's laugh surprised her. "Did you explain this to Jake that way? Believe me, the last thing any of the McCoys are afraid of is a little trouble."

Michelle managed a small smile. If she knew anything, she knew that. But she wouldn't, couldn't ask Jake to sacrifice any more for her than he already had. This was the only way she could guarantee he would remained untouched.

As Edgar had explained it to her, Jake was facing prison time for his part in this "whole charade." She smoothed her daughter's hair from her face, Lili's interest in her treat making her forget to push her away. If she gave herself up with no further fight, Edgar had agreed to leave Jake and his in-volvement in the entire matter out of it. But she, of course, would effectively be barred from ever entering the States again.

"He doesn't even know me," she found herself whispering.

Liz frowned, saying nothing for a long moment. "I'd bet you two know each other far better than either of you will admit to." She crossed her legs under the table. "Knowing someone sometimes has very little to do with knowing the minute details about each other's lives. If you're lucky, like Mitch and I are, it has to do with your *knowing* each other. Know what I mean?"

Michelle squinted at her. "In the...biblical sense?" she said, remembering the company of an impressionable four-year-old.

"Then there's that," Liz said, color warming her cheeks. "But no. What I mean is, without your having to say it, you know and he knows that what you share goes beyond the details. Details that were important before you met, but take on a whole new meaning afterward."

Michelle searched her face, trying to figure out what she was saying.

Liz sighed. "Okay, look, I'm still pretty new at all this love stuff myself. It took me most of my life to figure out that home isn't a place, but a person." She waved her hand. "But that's neither here nor there. What I want to tell you is that I've known all the McCoys for...well, for far longer than I'd like to admit to." Her smile told Michelle otherwise. "And Jake...well, Jake is never one to impulsively jump into anything. He's the type of guy who has his routines and never, I mean never, veers from them. Never, that is, until you."

Michelle averted her gaze, feeling her cheeks heat again. Liz's words made her remember her and Jake's first night together. Their long conversation about sex and his truckload of inhibitions...and her lack of them. She appreciated the irony of the situation. His argument that a couple should know each other better, that sex should be more than just a physical coming together, but that it had as much to do with respect and a general liking of the person you were sleeping with. Then there had been her counterargument that things like respect and liking had nothing to do with physical attraction.

Oh, how all that had changed, and quickly.

Liz was looking out the window as she continued. "I guess what I'm trying to say, Michelle, is this." She met her gaze. "Jake had more than the reasons you think to do what he did. He might have said he was marrying you to help you, but I suspect even he's coming to see what a lie that was." Her sudden smile seemed completely out of place. "As a matter of fact, I think he's already figured it out."

Michelle sensed his presence before she saw him. She turned her head to where he stood just inside the door, his gaze glued to her face.

Liz laid her hand on top of Michelle's where it laid on the table. "I can't tell you how much it must have taken him to come down here. Promise me one thing—that you'll hear him out."

Michelle nodded slowly.

Liz slipped from the booth. Lili had finished her pie and easily gave her hand to Liz when the woman offered to show her exactly how those little angels were made in the kitchen.

Michelle felt as though her heart had leaped up and was firmly lodged in her throat. But before she could say anything, the clang of a cowbell announced the arrival of another man.

Edgar Mollens.

Michelle bit on her lip as much to keep from crying out as to keep the tears from falling. Telling Jake once that she must leave had practically ripped her in two. To tell him goodbye again...

Her gaze fastened on his dear, dear face as he looked first at Edgar, then at her, his confused expression endearing him to her further. But the last thing she expected was the slow shaking of his head. No words. No protests. No declarations. Merely a simple gesture that said too much.

Edgar cleared his throat. "McCoy."

It seemed to take a moment for Jake to realize Edgar had spoken. "Mollens."

Edgar looked at Michelle meaningfully. "Your decision was the best possible one, Miss Lambert. You may not see that now, but rest assured, you will. And so will Jake."

"McCoy," Jake said quietly.

"What?" Edgar regarded Jake with a frown.

"I said McCoy. Her name's Mrs. McCoy." Jake didn't budge his gaze from Michelle's face as he said the words. "No matter what, we are married, Michelle. Your leaving won't change that. Not for me." He lifted his hand where his wedding band glinted in the afternoon light. "I'm married to you no matter where you are physically." His voice lowered to a gravelly roar. "I'd prefer it if you were here."

Edgar quickly stepped closer to Michelle. "Remember everything we talked about...Michelle. No matter if you leave now or two months from now, after all the legal red tape is out of the way, you will be leaving. The difference is whether Jake will go to prison or not. There's no way your marriage will stand up in a court of law. It'll fall apart like the house of cards it is within an hour of questioning."

Michelle looked from Jake to Edgar, her heart thudding painfully in her chest. *You're wrong,* she wanted to tell the INS agent. Hers and Jake's marriage was not a house of cards to be blown over with the lightest wind. While their union hadn't initially been based on love and permanent commitment, it had grown into that. And she suspected that rare were the times when young marriages could weather what hers and Jake's had in such a short period of time and manage to come out the stronger for it.

She glanced at her ringless finger. The absence of the simple wedding band meant little. Her bond to Jake transcended what a piece of jewelry could symbolize. She loved him, above and beyond nearly everything else in her life. She'd never thought herself capable of loving anyone other than her daughter for a long, long time, but from somewhere within, Jake had coaxed out a love that brimmed generously from her heart, filling it, filling her...bonding them.

Slowly, Jake began to lift his arms, inviting her into his embrace. With barely a hesitation, she slid from the booth and ran to him, burrowing into the soft folds of his sweatshirt, clutching him as if he were the four elements combined, everything in this world that she needed to survive.

"God forgive me for hurting you," she murmured, tilting her head to receive the kiss he pressed to the top of her head. "God forgive me for putting you through what you're going to face because of me. But I can't help myself. I love you, Jake McCoy."

Edgar muttered an especially crude curse. "You've just signed your death warrant, McCoy. Trust me on this. The company will never recognize your marriage."

Jake tucked Michelle tightly against his side and faced his co-worker. "You just go ahead and try to make this marriage look like anything less than a real marriage. You won't succeed. This is as solid as it gets. You're the one who's going to come away with something on the bottom of his shoes, Edgar."

The cowbell rang. Michelle looked up to see Melanie leading every last member of the McCoy family through the door like some sort of ragtag brigade. They were joined by the two men at the counter and the man with the cap in the kitchen. Liz rushed out on the cook's heels along with the other woman, then out came Lili. She bulleted to Michelle, tunneling her way between her and Jake, curving her thin arms around each of their legs.

Jake freed a hand and hesitantly reached down to touch Lili's blond curls. "You chose the wrong family to screw with, Edgar. No one ever crosses the McCoys."

_____ Epilogue _____

JAKE SNEAKED UP on his wife—_his wife_; how he loved calling Michelle that, with no reservations, no fears that their relationship didn't qualify—where she talked to his sisters-in-law, Liz and Melanie. He put his hands on her narrow waist and swiveled her to face him, the rustle of her wedding dress filling his ears, her flushed features and twinkling eyes filling his gaze. He'd never seen a woman look so beautiful. He wanted to tug her into the mammoth white tent set up in case of inclement weather, hoist her on top of one of the linen-covered tables and have at her right then and there.

But there were a hundred or so guests milling about the McCoy farm so he limited himself to a chaste taste of her sexy mouth.

He'd planned to ask her if she was happy but no longer felt the need to. The way she glowed in the setting sunlight that kissed her profile, practically floated over the neatly trimmed lawn in her puffy white dress, her laughter tinkling above the sound of silverware clinking against china, told him she _was_ happy. And it made him feel proud to know he was partially responsible.

It was difficult to believe it had been just three weeks ago that Michelle and Lili had been a heartbeat away from vanishing from his life. That the woman wriggling in his embrace had called Edgar Mollens and struck a deal that would get him off the hook with the INS.

So much had changed since then. Michelle and Lili had already transformed his apartment in Woodley Park into a home. Frilly curtains, colorful pillows, full cupboards and hoards of toys made it difficult to recognize the place when he came home at night. And he couldn't have been happier. Although he did have to talk to Michelle about the scruffy little cat Lili had brought home the day before.

"Hey, Jake, you know the rules," Melanie warned him. "No monopolizing the bride until after the reception."

Liz agreed. "That's right. You two are going to have plenty of time on your honeymoon."

The women fell silent, looking at a spot somewhere over his left shoulder. A man cleared his throat. Jake glanced to find Edgar standing awkwardly behind him and Michelle. His first instinct was to run, though running was no longer a concern.

Instead, he grinned, and he and Michelle turned to greet him. He extended his hand to his fellow agent. "Glad you could make it, Edgar."

"Yeah. Me, too." He glanced at Michelle. "Mrs. McCoy. Congratulations. You're a fetching bride."

Michelle's smile widened. "Thank you, Edgar."

Edgar's discomfort level seemed to grow the longer he stood there. He lifted a hand to his head and smoothed the little hair remaining there. "Look, I just wanted to, you know, apologize again for everything. And to give you this. Think of it as a wedding gift of sorts—except, of course, that you've earned it."

Michelle accepted the envelope.

"No need for apologies, Edgar. Funny thing is, you may be partially responsible for Michelle and me being where we are right now."

His wife's tiny gasp drew his attention. She slid out a brand-spanking-new green card. She looked at Jake, fresh tears making her eyes look that much brighter. Then she threw her arms around Edgar. "Thank you. Thank you so very much."

Edgar's face turned beet red. "It's nothing, really. Your coming in and explaining everything that happened in California ten years ago helped enormously. The review board unanimously decided you were no threat. From there, I didn't have any problem expediting things to get you this."

Jake pressed his lips against Michelle's ear. "Shall we forget Hawaii and make Paris our honeymoon destination, instead?"

Her answer was the closing of her eyes and a squeeze of his arm where it encircled her waist.

"Well...congratulations," Edgar said, ungracefully backing away and nearly tripping over a tent stake.

Liz and Mel immediately descended, wanting to see the new card that identified Michelle as a resident alien—though Jake didn't plan to stop until she was a full-fledged citizen. He caught a glimpse of Pops some distance behind his sisters-in-law, staring after the setting sun. The old man had been quieter than usual lately. And now, in the midst of the celebration, he couldn't have looked more melancholy.

Jake scanned the guests comprised of family, townsfolk and co-workers, until he spotted Mel's mother, Wilhemenia, straightening the hill of gifts on a nearby table.

Mel elbowed him in the ribs. "So are you going to leave us alone so we can indulge in some more girl talk or what, McCoy?"

Jake tore his gaze from Wilhemenia and held his hands up in surrender. "Okay, okay."

Michelle smiled. "Lili's in the barn, I think. Why don't you make sure she's not getting into any trouble."

Jake lifted her left hand and kissed the back, then reluctantly left his wife to continue her post-ceremony gossiping session. He caught Melanie saying something about Michelle's wedding ring, and his grin widened. He waved at David and Connor where they stood to the side clutching their long-neck beer bottles for dear life. The last two single McCoy brothers were obviously uncomfortable attending the third wedding reception for a McCoy in the past half year. Jake rounded the bandstand and navigated around one of several gas lamps. Ah, there she was.

Near the new barn, Mitch and Lili were feeding the livestock. His heart skipped a beat when Billy the Kid Goat licked Lili's palm, and she threw back her blond head and shrieked with laughter. Absently, Jake rubbed his leg.

In the past twenty-one days, he and Michelle and Lili had spent nearly every moment they could together as family. Except, of course, when he was at work, or when Lili took her afternoon naps and went to bed at night. It was then, when the little munchkin was otherwise occupied, that he and Michelle took advantage of every moment alone....

He looked at his monkey suit, longing for the jeans and oxford shirt he'd been wearing earlier in the day. Jeans. He couldn't remember the last time he'd worn a pair. But, as Michelle insisted, he looked damned good in them. He grinned. Well, he couldn't deny that they were more appropriate for a life that included a playful, messy four-year-old.

For the first few days after Michelle's decision to stay and fight the INS with him, he'd been torn as what to do. Quit his job? Or stay until everything was settled? He'd already pretty much guessed they wouldn't terminate his employment. Their reasons would have been shaky, at best. After all, the job of deporting Michelle had not been assigned to him, so conflict never entered the equation.

Now that she had her green card, he had to decide what he wanted to do. Something that helped potential immigrants, he thought. He and Mitch were already discussing the possibility of his buying into his P.I. partnership and including immigration and naturalization aid to their list of services.

And Michelle... Well, she had already been snapped up by a French restaurant within walking distance of their D.C. home, and her plans to open her own restaurant were already in the works.

"Jake!" Lili called, snapping him from his reverie.

He smiled and continued to the barn as she ran toward him. Even now, he acknowledged a tiny pang of awkwardness around the little girl. She was so...tiny. He, so large. But the pang instantly disappeared as she catapulted herself into his arms, giggling as he compensated for her weight by swinging her around. He crouched and straightened the skirt of her frilly dress. He couldn't be sure how much she understood of everything that had happened in the past three months. He planned to make the rest of her life as carefree and happy as possible.

"Did *Maman* tell you I talked to Nana and Grandpa this morning?" Lili said, speaking so quickly the words emerged as a single very long, breathy one.

Jake nodded, watching as Mitch gave him a wave then disappeared into the barn. "Yes, in fact, she did."

"They may be coming to visit me next month, did you know that?"

"Really?" He feigned ignorance, though he and Michelle had discussed the possible ramifications of their visit for the past three days. "That's great."

She hooked a finger inside the buttoned flap of his shirt and tugged. "Uh-huh." Her face screwed up into an expression that was becoming as familiar as her smile. It meant she was chewing something over. That she would share the thought was a forgone conclusion—another one of the qualities she'd inherited from her mother. "Since you and *Maman* are married, does that make you my papa?"

Jake tried not to cough at the sudden tickle in his throat. "That depends."

She frowned at him. "On what?"

He swept her bangs from her forehead with a brush of a finger. "On whether or not you want me to be."

She appeared to consider it long and hard. "Okay."

His chuckle vibrated straight down to his feet. "That easy, huh? 'Okay'?"

He hadn't heard Michelle approach, but her words were impossible to ignore. "She knows a good find when she comes across one." She came to stand between them. "Just like her mother."

Jake stood up, hiking a giggling Lili with him. Michelle locked her arms around them both and kissed Jake soundly on the cheek. Lili did the same on the other.

Jake closed his eyes and tightened his hold on both of them. He wasn't sure what he'd done, but it must have been something very good indeed to deserve the love of both of these special women.

Life just didn't get any better than this....

"So, shall we fly this joint?" Michelle whispered into his ear.

He chuckled, knowing she meant "blow this joint," but not caring. "Don't we have a couple of things to take care of first?"

He put Lili down, then took Michelle's hand as Lili tugged them to their guests. Liz clinked her glass several times until everyone settled down, then directed all the single men to gather for the tossing of the garter.

Jake eyed Michelle. He'd been aching to get under those yards of white material for hours. He only wished his family and most of Manchester weren't gathered to watch as he finally did so. To hoots and calls, he knelt and slowly slid her skirt up. He grinned at her surprised giggle and attempts to keep him from lifting it too far. But all laughter left him when he slipped a finger under the red and white garter, the flesh of her bare leg unbearably hot, air suddenly a rare commodity. It didn't matter how often he made love with this woman, every time was like the first time. Awkwardly, he drew the scrap of material down her leg. Once he finally had it free, he turned, twirling it around his index finger.

"Throw it, Papa!" Lili shouted from where Pops held her nearby. His throat tightened as he faced the small crowd of single men.

He chuckled when Marc and Mitch forced Connor and David to join the group, then stood as crossed-armed, smiling sentinels when the two bachelors tried to bolt. Turning, Jake gave the garter a squeeze, then flung it over his shoulder. A roar of laughter rippled through the gathering, and he turned to find the naughty bit of silk and lace sitting on top of the youngest McCoy's fair head. David dragged the garter from his hair and nearly tripped over his own feet when Connor punched him good-naturedly on the arm.

"The bouquet!" the waitress from the town's diner shouted. Bulleting her way through the throng of men, Myra waved her hands. "Do it just as we practiced, Michelle!"

Jake chuckled as he helped his wife to her feet.

But whatever the two women may or may not have practiced, the bouquet went far wide of the target of ten or so women gathered...and landed straight in Wilhemenia Weber's lap.

*It's hot...and it's out of control.
It's a two-alarm...*

BLAZE

**This summer, we're turning up the heat.
Look for these bold, provocative, ultra-sexy books!**

SHAMELESS by Kimberly Raye
July 2000

Deb Strickland has her hands full—keeping her
small-town newspaper in the black and her hands off
hunky Jimmy Mission. The sexy rancher has come
home to settle down—and that's definitely not in
Deb's plans. It looks like a case of unrequited lust—
until Jimmy makes Deb an offer she can't refuse.
An offer that's absolutely *shameless....*

RESTLESS by Kimberly Raye
November 2000

When bad boy Jack Mission returns home to
Inspiration, Texas, he promptly turns prim and proper
Paige Cassidy's life upside down. Divorced from a man
who swore she could do nothing right, Paige is on a
major self-improvement kick. And sexy, *restless* Jack
is just the man to give her a few lessons in love....

Don't miss this daring duo!

HARLEQUIN®

Temptation.

HARLEQUIN
Duets™

*Pick up a Harlequin Duets™
from August–October 2000
and receive $1.00 off the
original cover price.* *

*Experience the "lighter side of love"
in a Harlequin Duets™.
This unbeatable value just became
irresistible with our special introductory
price of $4.99 U.S./$5.99 CAN. for
2 Brand-New, Full-Length
Romantic Comedies.*

Offer available for a limited time only.
Offer applicable only to Harlequin Duets™.
*Original cover price is $5.99 U.S./$6.99 CAN.

If you enjoyed what you just read,
then we've got an offer you can't resist!

Take 2 bestselling
love stories FREE!
Plus get a FREE surprise gift!

COMING NEXT MONTH

#793 RULES OF ENGAGEMENT Jamie Denton

Jill Cassidy needs a fiancé—fast! Morgan Price needs a savvy lawyer—immediately! The gorgeous contractor agrees to pretend he's madly in love with her and attend her sister's wedding. In turn, Jill will settle his case. But drawing up the "rules of their engagement" brings trouble. For starters, they have to practice kissing. Then there's the single hotel room they *have* to share....

#794 GABE Lori Foster
The Buckhorn Brothers, Bk. 3

Gabe Kasper, the heartthrob of Buckhorn County, can have any woman he wants. But it's prickly, uptight college woman, Elizabeth Parks, who gets under his skin. She thinks Gabe's some kind of hero and wants an interview for her thesis. He doesn't consider pulling a couple of kids out of the lake heroic, but will answer her questions in exchange for kisses…and more.

#795 ALL THROUGH THE NIGHT Kate Hoffmann
Blaze

Is it love...or just a one-night stand? Advice columnist Nora Pierce can't answer that for sure. An unexpected night with warm sexy sportswriter Pete Beckett thrills her to the core. But the ex-jock is too laid back and a real ladies' man to boot. Nora can only read between the lines...and decide where to draw the line with Pete!

#796 SECRETLY YOURS Gina Wilkins
The Wild McBrides

Trent McBride is known for being brash, cocky and very, very reckless. But when a horrific plane crash leaves him grounded, he doesn't know what to do with his life. Then he meets spirited, *secretive* Annie Stewart and suddenly, he feels alive again. Especially when he learns that Annie desperately needs a hero....